BEFORE I FALL

Moore Friends Series

CELESTE GRANGER

Before I Fall, in the Moore Friends Series
Copyright 2019 Celeste Granger
All Rights Reserved and Proprietary.

Printed in the United States of America
Want to be in the know? Subscribe to my newsletter to be a part of Celeste Granger's Tangled Romance!
https://landing.mailerlite.com/webforms/landing/k2e1j4
Follow me on Facebook @ https://www.facebook.com/TheCelesteGranger/
Want to join my reading group, Reading with Celeste? Follow the link: https://www.facebook.com/groups/1943300475969127/

Acknowledgement

Gratitude…

It's the feeling I have every time I am able to put pen to paper and open my heart. That's where these characters you all have fallen in love with come from, my heart accompanied by my truest desire to tell a compelling story that draws you in, offering each reader a chance to fall in love, all over again. To say that I appreciate you is an understatement. Your unwavering support fuels me when I am tired and encourages me when the dearth of self-doubt rears its ugly head.

Thank you…

This story is dedicated to every bad girl who knows there is better just waiting for her.

Chapter One

"*A*nother late night, Sanaa?"

"Jealous much?" Sanaa clapped back.

Sanaa offered a falsified smile as she sashayed down the hallway of the Pinnacle Building in downtown Atlanta. The comment came from another one of Sanaa Chase's nameless male colleagues. Sanaa was surrounded by men, mostly older White men who found her dark brown skin, intriguing yet threatening at the same time. As one of the youngest stock traders in Pinnacle history, and as a Black woman, Sanaa Chase was an anomaly; unexpected and sometimes unwelcome. But one thing about Sanaa, she loved the challenge and the idea of conquest. There was nothing more satisfying than proving to the old boy's network that she did not come to play. She was worthy of the high six-figure salary she earned as well as the numerous accolades she received. The old boys were impressed by her, and many of them fantasized about Sanaa, whether they ever admitted it or not.

But Sanaa did have another late night, with her best friend, Tempestt Moore. As Sanaa settled into her corner office with panoramic views of the city, Sanaa sat in her executive chair and allowed her mind to wander as she gazed out of the window.

It was girl's night out at Masquerade, an adult only fantasy club that Sanaa discovered about a year ago. Masquerade was the perfect escape for Sanaa, especially after working long days with people who constantly challenged her reason for being there. True, Sanaa loved rising to a challenge, but even more, she appreciated a man who could rise to hers. Last night was that kind of night. His name was Nick or Rick, maybe Dick? Sanaa smiled as she thought back; crossing her long shapely leg and rocking her chair slightly from side to side. His name was irrelevant, but what Nick did? Memorable, certainly memorable.

The man was quick to caress her full breasts and pinch her nipples, making them taut. Pulling Sanaa even closer, the man wrapped his mouth around her plump breast and began to suckle as he fingered her other breast. Even as Sanaa looked out of the window, she could feel her breasts respond as though Nick was still there.

It didn't take long before Sanaa's internal temperature gauge registered hot. His mouth was warm, and his tongue was talented. When he gently bit down on Sanaa's pert nipple, a sexy whimper passed her lips. His mouth was warm, and his tongue was talented. Sanaa's mouth opened again, pausing on that same whimper. She instinctively tightened the press between her thighs as her yoni thumped in response.

"Excuse me, Ms. Chase?"

Chauncey had rapped lightly on the all-glass door to Ms. Chase's office and waited for her boss to acknowledge her. When Sanaa didn't, Chauncey rapped again before opening the door and calling out to her.

"Ms. Chase," Chauncey repeated taking a few passive steps in Sanaa's direction.

"Oh, Chauncey," Sanaa finally answered, swiveling her chair to face her executive assistant. "I didn't hear you."

"I see," Chauncey smiled tightly as she could see the

warmed flush of Sanaa's cheeks and the quickened rise and fall of Ms. Chase's chest. Sanaa saw how Chauncey looked at her and quickly resumed her professional posture in as much as she could. When Sanaa was promoted to lead trader last year, she was cognizant of her choice of assistant. She wanted to give another woman who looked like her an opportunity to be reflected in the male-dominated lily-white community Sanaa worked in. Chauncey Hines was a reflection of Sanaa and a poignant reminder to the men around Pinnacle that Sanaa might be the first, but she wouldn't be the last. To Sanaa, Chauncey was much more than her assistant. Sanaa made it her business to groom Chauncey to join her on the trading floor; giving her tips and insights into how the business of successful stock trading really worked. And Chauncey was an exceptional student, more than rising to the occasion. Soon, Chauncey would need to be replaced with another assistant, willing to take on the market and the trading culture as Chauncey made her ascent from assistant to first term trader.

"Just wanted to remind you about your ten o'clock meeting," Chauncey offered as she approached Sanaa's desk with the folder in hand. Sanaa accepted it knowing that it was the bullet point version of their most recent research on the client Sanaa would be meeting.

"Thank you, Chauncey," Sanaa replied. "And this morning, I need three espresso shots."

"Coming right up, Ms. Chase," Chauncey commented as she pivoted on her heels towards the door.

"Oh, and Chauncey? I want you to sit in on the meeting."

Chauncey spun around wearing a broad smile.

"Thank you, Ms. Chase!"

Sanaa smiled in return. Chauncey made haste in leaving the office. Getting her boss's coffee was regular, routine, but sitting in on such a pivotal meeting? That meant Sanaa's confidence in Chauncey's ability had grown significantly, and this client could be huge for Ms. Chase's portfolio, landing Sanaa firmly on the short list for partner. Chauncey's thoughts resembled Sanaa's as she fingered the folder, opening it to review the pertinent details inside. This could be the account that pushed her closer towards her goal.

KINGSTON PRIDED HIMSELF ON BEING ON TIME, AND THE WAY traffic was moving in Atlanta, Kingston was at risk of being late. That was intolerable, particularly in business. Even though the slow movement of traffic was aggravating, Kingston found himself smiling as he sat in the backseat of the chauffeur driven car, he rode in. His notions of timeliness were not his own and certainly not original. Kingston thought back to the multiple times he was reminded by his grandfather, the original Kingston Wells, about the importance of being on time. There was a slight uptick of Kingston's lips as he heard the gruff of his grandfather's voice during one of his many lectures on the importance of time.

"To be on time means to arrive fifteen minutes early. And to arrive at the appointed hour means you are late. That will never do," his grandfather would say. Although when Kingston first heard his namesake's commentary on the subject, he thought it was just another one of grandpa's little ditties. However, once Kingston became president and CEO of the family business, Kingston understood the importance of his grandpa's words implicitly. Losing his grandfather a few years ago was one of the hardest things Kingston ever endured. And even though to some it may appear to be a small thing, Kingston honored his grandfather's sage advice by being on time; his grandpa's definition of on time.

"Estimated time of arrival, Joel," Kingston asked from the back of the winter white Rolls Royce.

"Ten minutes, sir," Joel replied.

Kingston looked down at his Vacheron Constantin Tour de l'Ile timepiece, another nod to grandpa's time sensibilities. If all went to Joel's calculation, Kingston would arrive eighteen minutes early for his ten o'clock with Pinnacle. This was a meeting Kingston looked forward to. Although Wells Woods International had grown exponentially under Kingston III's tutelage, having a brokerage firm such as Pinnacle Unlimited as his mastiff would only serve to take his family's company to an even higher level. Kingston would not stop until Wells Woods International was the preeminent lumber industry in the world. Kingston's parents were exceptionally proud of their oldest child, having taken their initially small family business and causing such growth. Kingston intended to make his family even prouder. Partnering with Pinnacle and Sanaa Chase, specifically, was the vehicle to do just that. Kingston's eyes moved between the traffic and his watch as Joel masterfully moved the Rolls Royce through the crowded streets.

"Ms. Chase, Mr. Wells is here to see you," Chauncey announced. She was prepared with her notebook and laptop in hand. Sanaa nodded her acknowledgment, finishing the last of her espresso, popping in a mint, and checking her lip gloss before standing up. Sanaa was confident in her preparedness for the meeting. What others saw as her quick rise in the trading industry didn't take into account the many long nights; she spent doing the work others thought unnecessary. Sanaa studied potential clients, from their portfolio to their background to their social media presence. She felt it was important to be fluent when it came to her clientele; knowing as much about them as possible. Being armed with factual information placed Sanaa at a decided advantage. Because she had the facts, Sanaa could tell when a client was honest or when they tried to pull a fast one; whether they underestimated her ability or saw Sanaa for the powerhouse trader she was. Familiarity bred confidence in Sanaa's potential clients. A well-versed trader into their own profile busted their confidence that she would do the same in the negotiation of their collective endeavors.

"Mr. Wells," Sanaa announced as she entered the boardroom. Like a perfect gentleman, Kingston stood to his feet, lifting his six-foot-four-inch frame from the leather chair and extending a receptive hand, shaking Sanaa's. Kingston's eyes lingered as he felt a spark of magnetism as their hands connected. Like Sanaa, Kingston had done his homework. He'd seen pictures of Ms. Chase online and even live video of her in promotional advertisement for Pinnacle. Those images paled in comparison to the beauty that stood before him. Sanaa's touch was as gentle as her dark brown eyes. Yet, Kingston could see the spark of something more behind a veiled shadow, lurking in the depths of her mahogany brown pools. The bounce of Sanaa's naturally curly hair framed her beautiful face perfectly; highlighting Sanaa's flawless milk chocolate skin, pronounced cheekbones, and pouty full lips. Still, as Kingston's eyes took in the length of her, he had to stop himself from staring. Sanaa's statuesque and curvy frame was enough to turn heads and completely stop traffic.

Sanaa appreciated Kingston's elongated gaze as she had one of her own. Kingston's distinguished look was unmistakable from his neatly maintained low Caesar fade tapering down to his mocha almond skin, accentuated by a precisely trimmed mustache and beard to the broad of his nose and the perfection of his brilliant smile. There was another intriguing smile shared between the two when Kingston finally released Sanaa's hand. The prolonged handshake was not lost on Chauncey who remained in the background until their shared moment was over. As Sanaa took her seat, her eyes remained with Kingston, admiring the way his custom suit hung from his broad shoulders and flattered his athletic build.

"It's nice to meet you, Ms. Chase," Kingston replied as he waited until both ladies were seated before taking his chair once again. Sanaa liked the way Kingston's voice filled the boardroom; not because he spoke boisterously but the weight of his bass voice naturally resonated, echoing in Sanaa's ears and drumming rhythmically in her spirit. Sanaa would remember to fantasize about Kingston later, behind private doors, but for now, it was time to get down to business.

Chapter Two

"*M*r. Wells," Sanaa began, inclining herself in Kingston's direction as she crossed her long shapely legs.

"Let me start by saying, we appreciate you taking this meeting with Pinnacle."

"One small correction, if I may," Kingston crooned.

"Of course," Sanaa simmered.

"I'm taking this meeting with you, Ms. Chase."

There was that voice again. Sanaa's eyes closed momentarily as she allowed Kingston's phonic fortitude to wash over her. Sanaa's mink lashes fluttered as she opened her eyes, reestablishing contact with Mr. Wells.

"Appreciated," Sanaa purred with a delectable smile teetering on her full lips. There was a knowing smile shared between Kingston and Sanaa. Once again, Chauncey noticed. She was inclined to believe she knew the reason why which exceeded their natural attraction. In the past, the Pinnacle Group made several unsuccessful attempts to engage Wells Woods International. The company even trotted out their big guns to try and impress Kingston and his faction. However, Kingston was not moved or swayed by jargon they used that the Pinnacle Group hoped was over Kingston's young head. They didn't take him seriously as he was the heir apparent to the then-burgeoning company. The big guns made the mistake of assuming because Wells Woods was a family business run by the previous CEO's son, that Kingston was somehow a figurehead and not a real force to be reckoned with. Mr. Wells allowed their prepubescent thoughts to stand, refusing to do business with the well-established trading company. Kingston didn't care what they thought of him personally. However, he refused to have the powers that be discount the value and validity of his company.

That was until Kingston met Ms. Chase. Their initial encounter was completely by happenstance. They both happened to be at the same place at the same time, on business that was of mutual interest. Kingston was philanthropic. Because of his lineage, Kingston was fortunate in that he never had to worry about money. That didn't mean Kingston didn't have to work hard. His grandfather and his father insisted that Kingston III work his way up through the company, learning every facet firsthand, as well as learning about the individuals employed by the company. Even when Wells Woods was in the early stages, being the only minority-owned lumber company offered specific advantages. Companies, whether government or private, were afforded incentives and particular tax-breaks when contracting with minority companies. What had been historically held against people of color worked to the Wells company advantage. With those contracts came recognition for exemplary work. One good contract led to the maintenance of those initial ones as well as the acquisition of many others. But there was another facet of Kingston's philanthropy many weren't aware of. The lumber industry could be seen as a destructive force. Their money was made from cutting down trees. Kingston didn't want just to take away from the environment. He also wanted to restore it. as an anonymous donor, Kingston ensured that international geographical locations that suffered natural disasters, as well as unscrupulous destruction of forests and green spaces, were restored by the donation of hundreds of thousands of trees worldwide.

Sanaa and Kingston attended a gala for Habitat for Humanity Atlanta. Wells Woods contributed the lumber to build one hundred homes in Atlanta and surrounding areas while. Sanaa was there not as a representative of Pinnacle but representing her own philanthropic endeavors. Helping the homeless was more than a nice thing to do, for Sanaa. She knew what it was like to be without a roof over her head and a warm place to sleep. Being homeless was a part of Sanaa's past that she would just as soon forget yet forgetting was impossible. Sanaa spent time on the streets as a teenager, troubled by her past while desperately trying to hold onto hope for what she dreamed for her future — those years vying for a safe place to sleep shaped Sanaa in ways she couldn't deny and learned to appreciate. Sanaa learned self-protection being on the street because there was no one else there to protect her. She learned survival being on her own. Sanaa learned tenacity and cunning from the streets. That tenacity spilled over into her the way Sanaa conducted business. Being cunning infiltrated every facet of Sanaa's life.

Kingston and Sanaa moved in the same space. Sanaa made sure her orbit connected succinctly with Kingston's. She knew of Pinnacle's failed history with Wells International. Sanaa also knew that trying to hard sell Mr. Wells on the company that previously insulted him would not work. Sanaa ensured that when she approached Kingston, she did so appealing to his heart, his pension for helping those less fortunate. Admittedly, Kingston was impressed by Sanaa. In their brief encounter, Kingston learned two things. Not only was Sanaa Chase breathtakingly beautiful, but she was also intelligent, with a business accouterment not to be trifled with.

Kingston was intrigued. That intrigue continued to their inevitable intentional encounter.

"Ms. Chase, I have reviewed your proposition for representation for my company, and I must say, the numbers you posit are ambitious, to say the least," Kingston suggested.

"Mr. Wells," Sanaa began, her voice musically tickling Kingston's ears. "There's a reason why we are here together. And as you said, you are doing business with me. If my numbers were not rock solid, founded on not only empirically proven statistical analysis but my unwavering gut, bolstered by my confidence in what Wells Woods International has to offer, there would be no point to this meeting." Sanaa leaned forward in her chair, slowly lacing her fingers together and resting them on the tiger wood table. "Mr. Wells, I didn't come to play. I came to impress."

Kingston allowed his eyes to fall to the figures in front of him once again. But he was drawn back to the enticing gaze of Sanaa.

"That you did not," he chortled.

Chauncey took precarious notes, but not the ones she needed to record either on her tablet or notepad. Just as Kingston studied Sanaa, so did Chauncey. She took note of how Sanaa leveled her intelligence; not to intimidate but to inspire. Chauncey appreciated how Sanaa used her feminine proclivities to covertly engage without overt flirtation. Chauncey was glad she was there to bear witness to the real art of negotiation.

"I'm glad you're pleased, Mr. Wells," Sanaa chimed.

"Please, call me Kingston."

"I will," Sanaa smiled, "after you sign on the dotted line."

Sanaa lifted the Mont Blanc pen from inside her leather portfolio, along with the official contract between the Pinnacle Group and Wells Woods International. Her extension of the pen was well received. Kingston happily signed on the dotted line, sealing a multimillion-dollar engagement. When

Kingston returned the pen to Sanaa, their hands touched once again. The contact was not inadvertent. Kingston intended it. His need to make physical contact with Sanaa was more than compulsion. He was drawn to her; his attraction greater than a moth to a flashing hot flame. The pulsing sensation Sanaa experienced in hearing Kingston's voice was a mere precursor to what his touch did to her. It was a titillating experience Sanaa couldn't quell.

"Thank you, Kingston," Sanaa replied, taking the pen from his hand and signing her name on the legal document. There was a daring smile that lingered on the turn of Kingston's lips. He loved how his name sounded articulating from Sanaa's pouty lips.

"We should celebrate," Kingston suggested, closing his portfolio and resting back in his chair.

"Thanks for the offer, Mr. Wells, but I don't mix business with pleasure," Sanaa quipped. There was a sensual smile that danced on her lips. Part of what Sanaa said wasn't true. She intended to mix business with pleasure but outside of the presence of the man who captivated her attention. She would have her way with Kingston; however, he would be none the wiser.

"That's where you're wrong, Ms. Chase," Kingston began. "We wouldn't be mixing business with pleasure. Our celebration would be solely pleasure."

Chauncey dreamily placed a hand to her flushing cheek. Although Mr. Wells comment was not directed towards her, she felt the power of his scintillating words.

Sanaa eyed Kingston unashamedly. Her intention for the meeting had already been accomplished. Sanaa had nothing to lose by engaging in a bit of pleasure with Kingston. Besides, doing so fit her modus operandi. Sanaa wasn't into meaningful encounters. Sanaa was into pleasing ones.

"In that case," Sanaa began; the devilish grin spreading across her full lips. Sanaa extended an upturned hand in

Kington's direction. A single thick brow lifted on his handsome face as he extended his hand in return. Picking up the Mont Blanc, Sanaa wrote her cell phone number in Kingston's palm. When she was done, Sanaa stood up from the table and pivoted on her four-inch black on black Jimmy Choo's. seeing Sanaa's power move, Chauncey stood up as well. She fell in line behind her boss unconsciously mimicking Sanaa's sway. Kingston smiled looking down at the number on his hand. But he didn't miss Sanaa's exit from the room. That, he would never miss.

Chapter Three

"*W*ell," a familiar voice said on the line.

"Well, what," Sanaa smiled kicking off her shoes and sitting down her clutch on the hallway table in her condo.

"Bestie, do not play with me," Tempestt playfully threatened. "Did you land the lumber king or not?"

Sanaa's hand eased up riding the curve of her hip. "Tempestt Moore, did you doubt me," Sanaa quipped. "I thought you knew better!"

"Hey now! That's my girl!"

"That's more like it," Sanaa sang. "Doubting me, tuh."

"I am so proud of you, Sanaa," Tempestt smiled.

Sanaa knew Tempestt's sentiments were sincere. Tempestt had been Sanaa's rock for a long time. She was more than a best friend. Tempestt was more like a sister. When Sanaa was at her lowest, unsure of herself, unsure of her place in the world, Tempestt was there reassuring her that everything would work out just the way it was supposed to. Just as importantly, Tempestt never judged Sanaa, no matter what dangerously adventurous trouble Sanaa managed to get herself into. Tempestt had even gone so far as to get into some carnally risqué exploits of her own, landing Tempestt the man she loved. That was good for Tempestt and Sanaa didn't hold that against her. It's just not what Sanaa was looking for.

"Thank you, girl," Sanaa replied, strolling into the kitchen. After a long but fruitful day, Sanaa took out a bottle of scotch. Securing a shot glass from the cupboard, Sanaa opened the bottle and made a three-finger pour.

"So, how do you want to celebrate your wonderful accomplishment," Tempestt asked. Celebrating with her bestie was as much tradition as Sanaa's shot of scotch. "I know you made enough money on this deal to treat me nice," Tempestt teased. "But, since we are celebrating you, I guess I can pay."

"You know what I want," Sanaa chortled.

"Seriously, Sanaa," Tempestt hissed.

"Damn straight," Sanaa snapped. "Ain't nothin' changed, more money or not," she continued.

"Fine," Tempestt begrudgingly agreed. "Pecan pancakes it is," she answered. "Are you coming over tonight?"

"Well," Sanaa chimed.

"You did not!"

Sanaa threw her head back and laughed and then quickly covered her mouth waiting for the commentary that was sure to come.

"Didn't you tell me you were turning over a new leaf for the new year? Don't answer that," Tempestt commented. "We are barely into the new year, and already you've gone back on what you said? Now you know I would never judge you for your sexual calisthenics with your nameless conquests. Judging is not what I do," Tempestt fussed. "But come on Sanaa! I held out hope that you would hold out at least until spring."

"I couldn't help it," Sanaa giggled.

"Oh, I'm so sure you couldn't," Tempestt sighed.

"So, when are you going to see the lumber king?"

"In just a little while," Sanaa laughingly admitted.

"Fine," Tempestt acquiesced. "But have your ass at my

place in the morning. I want every detail before you get your pancakes."

"I promise," Sanaa smiled. "Love you, Tempestt."

"Mmhmm," Tempestt hummed. "I will see you in the morning. And don't you dare be late."

"Never."

Sanaa and Tempestt ended the call. After sitting down her cell phone on the granite countertop, Sanaa lifted the shot glass, toasting herself.

"Way to go, baby girl," Sanaa announced and then downed the shot. She gasped as she felt the warm burn of the dark liquor descending her throat and resting in her belly.

"Whew."

Sanaa rubbed her stomach as she padded into her bedroom. She needed to remove all evidence of the day and rest for a while before going out with Kingston. Maybe she would take Mr. Wells to Masquerade?

Nah, Sanaa said to herself as she started to undress. Masquerade was for the brave, the uninhibited. Sanaa didn't know enough about Kingston to decide if he was right for the exclusive club. Maybe Kingston was a sexual prude. The thought of that made Sanaa laugh out loud. Kingston was so easy on the eye; she couldn't imagine that he would be sexually reclusive. Yet, there had been other equally provocative men that turned out to be boring as hell in bed; straight missionary position, no flavor. For them, daring was hitting it from the back. Sanaa shook her head, smiling sarcastically at the memory. She would be able to tell, soon enough whether Kingston was up to it or not. Stepping out of her pants and draping them casually across the footboard of her bed, Sanaa meandered over to the walk-in closet.

"Whatever shall I wear," Sanaa contemplated as she ran her fingers over her extensive wardrobe. Although Sanaa intended to test the limits with Kingston, feel him out, as it were, she didn't want her outfit to scream it. She needed to be alluring but not pornographic, showing just enough skin to heighten the intrigue, but not so much that there was nothing left to Kingston's imagination.

Once Kingston was settled into his hotel, the next order of business was getting in contact with Sanaa. He hadn't stopped thinking about her since leaving the offices of the Pinnacle Group. There was just something about Sanaa that Kingston couldn't quite put his finger on, yet, he was determined to find out. Kingston got a small taste of it during their initial meeting. Sitting across the boardroom table from Sanaa did more than whet his appetite. Still, Kingston desired more.

Sanaa wasn't surprised when her cell phone rang. Attracting men was never a problem for Sanaa. She'd always been capable of animalistic attraction. It was human nature. Most men could not resist a beautiful woman. Sanaa wasn't cocky about her looks. She learned, however, to be confident and use what God had given her to her greatest advantage. Her looks caused enough disadvantage in her life. When a young girl's developed body defies her age, men notice the womanly changes. Age didn't matter; hell, connection didn't matter. And when a young girl tells her mother that a grown man, her mother's boyfriend, Joe, came on to her, trying to touch her in ways that made her scared and uncomfortable, that young girl looks to her mother to take care of her. But she didn't. Sanaa's mother didn't believe that her old man was attracted to Sanaa; that Joe tried to sweet talk her, tried to touch her blossoming breasts and newly curvy hips. Instead of siding with her only daughter, Sanaa's mom accused her daughter of being fast; somehow making the old man's actions Sanaa's fault. Her mother didn't protect her. Sanaa's mother blamed her. Everything changed after that. Sanaa chose the street over staying where she wasn't loved; where her essence was threatened, where she wasn't protected.

Unfortunately, or fortunately, depending on perspective, Sanaa learned about male-female connection much earlier than she should have. The difficulty Sanaa had was discerning good connections from bad. Although Sanaa may have used her looks to attract men, she didn't like the natural fall out of mere physical attraction. On the face of it, Sanaa intended to enjoy the company of a man and nothing more. And she was good at it, to a certain degree. The problem was those times when more than her body was involved. Things got convoluted and unnecessarily complicated when Sanaa's heart was pricked. She'd walled her emotions away in her youth, as a safety measure. The heart made her weak and vulnerable to things and situations that only hurt her in the long run. Sanaa vowed that she would never voluntarily open herself up to pain again. For the most part, Sanaa had been successful, just about as successful as she had been in her business endeavors. But, there were those entanglements that exceeded what Sanaa intended that did hurt her in the end. Those painful reminders set new, stronger stones encamped around Sanaa's heart; walling off her vulnerabilities and fortifying her resolve. She'd become impenetrable, in a manner of speaking. She intended the same with Kingston Wells III.

"Sanaa," Kingston strummed.

"Good afternoon, Kingston."

"I'm glad you took my call," he replied.

"Did you think I wouldn't," Sanaa purred.

"Well," Kingston answered.

"What you will learn very quickly is that I'm no tease. I say what I mean, and mean precisely what I say," Sanaa clarified.

"I will hold you to that," Kingston crooned. Sanaa could hear the smile infiltrating his sensual lips. She had to keep it cool though. His voice was doing that thing to her again. Even over the phone, the melodic sensation of Kingston's voice was an instant panty dropper.

You can hold a hell of a lot more than that, Sanaa thought but didn't say.

"I expect nothing less," she did say.

"What time shall I pick you up," Kingston asked.

"I'm more of a meet you there kind of girl," Sanaa replied. She couldn't appear too easy and certainly not gullible.

"Just in case," Kingston suggested.

Yes, just in case," Sanaa answered.

Her suggestion didn't meet with Kingston's original plan. Although he understood Sanaa's reasoning, Kingston preferred to be a gentleman and pick her up for their date. However, he wanted Sanaa to be comfortable, and so he would concede, this time.

"Okay," Kingston began, "I understand," he continued. "I'll text location and time if that's good with you?"

"That's perfect."

"Excellent. I'll see you soon."

Chapter Four

*W*hen Sanaa received the text, she smiled. The restaurant Kingston picked was one that she'd been to before and enjoyed immensely. Situated on the uppermost floor of the Peachtree Plaza Westin, the Sun Dial, famous for the slow rotation the restaurant makes while dinner is served, is a hallmark in Atlanta. The luxurious accommodations, five-star menu, and observatory level, offering a panoramic view of 360 degrees, perched over seven hundred feet above the city, showcases seamless views of the city's amazing skyline. The Sun Dial was both classy and impressive, and knowing their destination gave Sanaa just the right insight as to what she should wear. She smiled as she read the side note at the bottom of Kingston's text.

Since you're going to meet me there, the least I can do is send a car.

Unlike Kingston, Sanaa didn't have the same kind of inclinations regarding time. She had no problem making the driver wait. By the time Sanaa sashayed to the car waiting for her, she was a fashionable fifteen minutes behind schedule. By the time Sanaa arrived at the Sun Dial, she was a half hour late. Kingston would have to forgive her. When Sanaa exited the elevator on the penthouse floor, the pensive impatient look in Kingston's eyes quickly faded away once she came into view. Kingston stopped mid-pace, turning his full attention to Sanaa. The coat check was there to assist in removing the faux fur stole that shielded Sanaa from the cool of the evening. Kingston's eyes widened as he took Sanaa in, allowing his eyes to travel the length of her. The red off the shoulder, mermaid cut dress hugged Sanaa's every voluptuous curve and flared slightly near her toned calves. The silver clutch matched the five-inch Miu Miu peep-toe stilettoes that adorned Sanaa's pedicured feet.

"Wow," Kingston sighed stepping forward. "Sanaa, you look amazing."

"Thank you," Sanaa smiled, looking up into Kingston's onyx eyes.

"I'm sure you hear that all the time," Kingston suggested as he lifted his arm to escort her.

"Not all the time," Sanaa smiled. She laced her arm around the strength of Kingston's and allowed him to lead her into the restaurant. They must have appeared to be a striking couple as every eye turned as they made their way to the table. Kingston must have used his influence as they sat at the most prominent table in the restaurant with the greatest viewpoint.

In line with The Sun Dial's reputation for service, the wine Sommelier arrived shortly after the waiter proffered menus for the guests. Kingston smiled as he gazed around the room. Despite the amazing views, many eyes were still on Sanaa.

"Good evening, madam, sir," the Sommelier began. "Shall I review the house wines for you?"

"Thank you," Kingston replied.

"Tonight, the Sun Dial is offering the 2014 Kathy Hall Cabernet. For the white option, we have Armand de Brignac Ace of Spades, and lastly, the Catena Zapata Adrianna Vineyard White Bones, 2015."

"Sanaa, do you have a preference," Kingston asked.

"I'll leave the selection up to you, Kingston."

"We'll have the Armand de Brignac," Kingston replied.

The Sommelier returned, pouring a small amount of the wine into Mr. Wells' glass for final approval before serving. Expertly, Kingston swirled the wine in his glass appreciating the color. Sanaa looked on interestedly as Kingston first sniffed then tasted the offering. With a nod, Kingston gave his approval, and the Sommelier responded by filling both glasses. Kingston awaited Sanaa's approval of his selection. He watched as her lips graced the edge of the glass and Sanaa's eyes lowered as she lifted the wine to her mouth. Kingston's eyes narrowed as Sanaa swallowed, folding her lips in slightly before releasing them, restoring their original fullness.

"Does the wine meet with your approval," Kingston asked, his eyes still focused on the sexy of Sanaa's mouth.

"It does," she smiled.

Her smile pleased him.

Over a delicious dinner of a baby wedge salad, the Sun Dial's signature butter poached lobster bake served over heirloom orange grits, with baby carrots and cream corn sauce, the conversation between Kingston and Sanaa was a natural extension of their earlier meeting. Talking business was comfortable for them both; not too intrusive, not too revealing, but interesting, nonetheless.

"Tell me Kingston, what's next for Wells Woods?"

"We are always interested in expansion," Kingston replied, resting his back on the chair. "Our research and development team has designed new modular furniture options that would benefit developing nations where internal space is limited and needs to be maximized for optimal living."

"That's admirable," Sanaa replied. "So, your charitable endeavors are not limited to Habitat for Humanity."

Kingston smiled. He was reminded of their first encounter and the beginning of his intrigue with Sanaa Chase.

"No, Sanaa, they are not," Kingston answered. "Positioning the company in the market is as much about tradition and innovation as it is about aiding and assisting. I wouldn't have it any other way."

"There's a reason for that," Sanaa suggested.

"There is," Kington admitted. "But enough about me," he began. "I would love nothing more than to stroll to the observation level and learn more about you. Will you join me?"

"Of course," Sanaa replied. "I love the observation deck."

"But not my inquiry," Kingston asked as he stood to his feet.

"We'll see," Sanaa quipped accepting Kingston pulling out her chair.

The observation layer was breathtaking as the lights of the skyline poised a beautiful juxtaposition to the dark of the sky itself. Kingston and Sanaa sipped champagne as they gazed out of the unobstructed window, with the floor moving ever so slightly under their feet.

"Tell me, Sanaa, what drew you to stock trading," Kingston asked refocusing his attention on the one who mattered more than the view.

"Power, control, risk," Sanaa quickly replied. Kingston saw Sanaa's eyes light up passionately as she spoke. "To know that I can influence fortunes based on my intellect and prowess? It's exhilarating," Sanaa purred.

"Is there anything else you're passionate about," Kingston crooned as he gazed down into Sanaa's alluring eyes.

"Maybe," Sanaa simpered with a wink. When Sanaa took a step forward, Kingston did the same. Now they were peering at each other; Kingston's eyes were hooded and penetrating, Sanaa's eyes were dazzling and tempting. It felt like there was a magnetic field encamped around them, drawing one to the other. Yet, the pull was as much internal as it was external. The initial attraction seemed to have morphed into something more.

Kingston's unyielding gaze was galvanizing, sending heated tremors to Sanaa's core. Sanaa tried to deny the pulsing knot in her stomach and the rapid beat of her heart. Those things were feelings based, emotionally driven. Kingston pulled Sanaa into him with a strong arm and a firm hand to the center of her back. Sanaa moved in without hesitation; curiosity as to his veracity getting the best of her. A pulsating flutter rose at the base of Sanaa's neck as Kingston's strong but gentle hand cupped her there, inclining her head to him as his lips feather kissed hers before demanding more. Their lips connecting seemed almost inevitable. It was the culmination of the rising sexual tension, the titillating teasing, and the base carnal instinct that neither could steer clear of. Sanaa was unpleasantly surprised at the touch of Kingston's lips. It piqued something in her that registered more than just between her thighs.

Shut that shit down Naa; she scolded herself as Kingston eased his lips away from her and then followed such an impassioned kiss with a sweet one on the tip of her nose, leaving a final sweet kiss to Sanaa's forehead. The gentleness of Kingston's kiss did not follow what Sanaa anticipated. It was confusing and curious. Sanaa expected Kingston to act like every other man who got close enough to feel her essence. She expected him to be ravenous. She expected to feel the swell of Kingston's dick pressing against her belly. She expected him to claw at her breasts and grab her ass, lured by her irresistible body. Why wouldn't she? Joe was tempted when Sanaa was young and barely blossoming. Now that Sanaa had grown into her femininity and her full self, why wouldn't Kingston be carnally tempted too?

Maybe he was, Sanaa thought. Maybe the public nature of where they were precluded Kingston from acting on what she knew his body wanted. Besides, Kingston was just a man, like any other. But even after they left the Sun Dial and went for a nightcap at the very popular U-Bar, Kingston remained the perfect gentleman; despite Sanaa's not so clandestine effort to see what he was really made of. The DJ had the U-Bar jumping.

"Hey beautiful, would you like to dance?"

It wasn't Kingston who asked Sanaa. When she turned on the bar stool and peered up, it was another handsome man making the request. Sanaa's eyes traveled to Kington to see what his response would be. He had no real claim on Sanaa. She wanted to see if the request of another would compel one.

"Sure, I would love to," Sanaa said to the man who approached her. He extended his hand and Sanaa accepted, falling in step behind him and sauntering to the dance floor. She felt Kingston's eyes on her, and with a casual look over the shoulder, Sanaa confirmed that Kingston couldn't keep his eyes off her. Smilingly, Sanaa turned her attention to the tall, dark and handsome man that stood before her. He was sexy enough, and the slow grind of the dancer's hips moved Sanaa in the same way. Her arms moved rhythmically over her head as the man danced behind her moving with the sway of Sanaa's hips, transfixed as she thought Kingston would be. Still, even on the dance floor, Sanaa felt Kingston's never yielding gaze, drinking her in from a distance. Although she moved in sync with the handsome stranger, Sanaa danced for Kingston alone.

Kingston felt that same cosmetic transcendental pull. There was an incredible tug on Kingston's heart, one he'd never felt before. He needed answers, but Kingston had no desire to rush in; to read incorrectly what he thought were signs. He'd done that before; mistaking hopefulness for real-ness. Kingston had no intentions of making the same mistake again. Still, he couldn't take his eyes off Sanaa. His feet moved in her direction even before Kingston had conscious thought of it. Kingston's stride was strong and forthright. He only had eyes for Sanaa although there were plenty of women who had eyes for him. She saw Kingston crossing the dance floor, moving determinedly yet suavely in her direction. A lascivious smile tilted the corners of Sanaa's pouty lips. Her hips dipped low, undulating in response to the deep bass beat. Sanaa's eyes never left Kingston as he smoothly closed the distance between them. When he stood in front of her, Kingston made his intentions clear; not just to Sanaa but to the man dancing behind her. Kingston didn't have to say a word. The dominance of his presence was enough.

Being this close to her, under the cover of mesmerizing darkness with syncopated beats fueling their movements, Sanaa would see who Kingston really was. His touch was claiming but not groping; protective but not possessive; comforting not violating. Sanaa traced a single finger down Kingston's center, stopping just short of grazing the manliness she knew existed between his muscular thighs. Masterfully, Kingston lifted Sanaa's hands moving it higher on his chest as their bodies continued to sway in motion.

And even as they stood at the entrance to Sanaa's home, a relinquishment of her earlier position, Kingston still remained honorable.

"I enjoyed myself tonight," Kingston began. "I hope you did as well, Sanaa?"

"I did," Sanaa sang. "But the enjoyment doesn't have to end at my doorstep," Sanaa teased. Again, she lifted her finger, slowly and deliberately tracing the broad of Kingston's nose, lingering on his lips, down the length of his neck to his broad chest and down the center of his core. Their eyes locked as Sanaa's finger continued to move; outlining the top of Kingston's tailored slacks, the hook of his belt buckle and the start of his zipper.

"Eh," Kingston started. But his words were halted when his lips were captured with a heated probing kiss. Sanaa thrust her tongue in Kingston's mouth, exploring him, imploring his masculine response. Yet, in the midst, Kingston stopped her hand from moving further and eased away from Sanaa's hot kiss. Sanaa's eyes were wide behind the hesitation. She gazed into Kingston's searching for the man she knew from her past; all the men she knew who only wanted Sanaa for her body. When she didn't see lust reflected in Kingston's eyes, Sanaa was perplexed.

"Sanaa, beloved, I am attracted to you," Kingston began, his voice soothing. "And I want to get to know you, I do," he continued. "But let's not rush things. I don't want to ruin what could be. Do you understand?"

Sanaa wanted to say no, that she didn't understand because she didn't. Kingston's words and his actions defied everything Sanaa had come to know to be true. Kingston watched until he saw a semblance of softness come to Sanaa's eyes.

"Good night, beloved," Kingston smiled, kissing Sanaa gently on the forehead. "I'll talk to you soon."

Sanaa's brow furrowed despite his gentle touch. She was miffed and perplexed. Kingston started down the sidewalk but waited until Sanaa was safely inside before getting into the car. From the side panel of her front door, Sanaa watched until Kingston drove away.

Chapter Five

"*Y*ou're late," Tempestt fussed. "It's a good thing I didn't put the pancakes on the griddle."

Tempestt expected a quick clap back from Sanaa. When she didn't get one, Tempestt turned around. Something wasn't right with Sanaa. The wrinkle of her brow and the look in Sanaa's eyes said so.

"What's the matter, Sanaa?"

Sanaa had Tempestt full attention. "Did something happen? Did the lumber king do something to you?"

"That's the problem," Sanaa began; her voice dry and emotionless. "He didn't do a damn thing to me, no matter what I tried."

Now Tempestt was the one with the furrowed brow. "I don't think I understand."

"Is it too early for a drink," Sanaa huffed.

"I've made mimosas," Tempestt answered.

"Juice won't do it," Sanaa rebuffed. "I need something stronger, darker."

Tempestt looked over at the clock and then back at Sanaa.

"I guess it's five o'clock somewhere," Tempestt sighed. She didn't like Sanaa's affect. She wasn't her feisty, perky self. If liquor would help Sanaa to talk, then Tempestt would oblige. Tempestt crossed the kitchen and traipsed into the den retrieving a bottle of Hennessey. Drinking hard liquor wasn't something she did too often, but Tempestt was willing to make the exception for her bestie. By the time Tempestt returned to the kitchen, Sanaa had already gotten up and retrieved two glasses from the cabinet, sitting them on the table.

"You're ready for this, huh," Tempestt asked, sitting the bottle down. Sanaa didn't reply. Instead, she reached for the bottle and after opening it, poured two hefty shots in the glasses. By the time Tempestt took a seat and picked up her glass, Sanaa was already gulping down her shot. Tempestt shook her head when Sanaa sat the glass down empty and poured herself another. Tempestt lifted her glass taking a sip. Sanaa took another gulp from her glass and set it down again.

"Are you ready to talk now," Tempestt asked. She didn't want Sanaa to get drunk or sick from drinking too fast. Getting her talking may be the only way to avoid that. Sanaa shook her head and then rested her chin in her hand.

"Oh, we gonc talk about this," Tempestt said insistently. "Tell me what happened? Was the guy that bad?"

"He was the exact opposite, Temp," Sanaa gruffed.

"So, he was good?" Tempestt questioned, wrinkling her brow more as well as her nose. She hadn't drunk that much so Tempestt knew she wasn't tripping.

"Yes!" Sanaa barked. "That's exactly it! That mother-fucker was good, too good."

"And that's a problem because," Tempestt queried.

"Because I don't do good," Sanaa complained. "Good is complicated. It requires too much."

Tempestt didn't immediately ask another question. She sat with what Sanaa said, doing her best to understand it. The two had been friends for years, an unlikely pair, but real friends, nonetheless. A part of what Sanaa said made some sense to Tempestt. She knew what Sanaa had been through;

her past hurts, the barriers Sanaa created to insulate herself.
On the outside, Sanaa looked like an accomplished woman,
and she was on many levels. But Tempestt knew that on the
inside, Sanaa was still that little girl who wanted her mom to
believe her when she told her about the bad man.

The bad man…

It all made sense.

Sanaa finished her drink and reached for the bottle again.

"Uhn," Tempestt said, pulling the bottle out of range.

"Come on, Temp. I need this," Sanaa whined.

"No, you need to talk this shit through."

"What's talking gone do? He good. More importantly, I'm
good, and if I'm not, I will be, hell. I don't like that shit.
Next!" Sanaa feigned like it was no big deal, but she was
fuming.

"As much as I love you Sanaa, that's the dumbest shit I've
ever heard you say out loud."

"Makes sense to me," Sanaa insisted.

"That's the problem though," Tempestt interjected.
"Which part of you does it make sense to?"

"What the hell does that mean," Sanaa winced. "The
whole part," she replied, tracing her silhouette with both
hands. "The whole part."

Tempestt exhaled deeply; her shoulders folding in on
themselves. "I know you ain't gone want to hear this Sanaa,
but I'm gonna say it anyway."

"No lecture, Tempestt. Pleaassse."

"You are getting this lecture," Tempestt clapped back. She
didn't even respond when Sanaa rested her elbows on the
counter and then her head in both hands like she was bored.

"I get it that for you good is bad, but have you considered,
Sanaa, that there is more to life than sexual conquests, anonymous romps in the sack, and hating yourself afterward for it?"

"Who said I feel some kind of way afterward?"

"I do, Sanaa! Did you forget who you're talking to? How

many morning after's have we been together, huh? How many, Sanaa?"

Sanaa rolled her eyes but didn't answer.

"Exactly! That's why I know that even though you think you want bad and uncomplicated, what you secretly desire is good and complicated."

"You're just saying that because you have Xavier," Sanaa protested.

"No, that's not at all why," Tempestt sighed. "You, my friend, are still angry. You think you are hurting those who hurt you by doing what you're doing, not making true connections. But don't you see, Sanaa, by not making real connections, you are repeating the same sad cycle? You are repeating the disconnection you felt with your mother and emulating the connection you thought she had with Joe or whatever that bastards name was."

Sanaa was quiet, and her bottom lip was poked out like a two-year-old toddler who heard no for the umpteenth time but still thought the pouty face would work.

"You think you're smart, dontcha?"

"Not if what I said doesn't make sense to you," Tempestt answered. "All of you," she giggled, mimicking the silhouette move Sanaa made earlier.

"You make me so sick," Sanaa groaned.

"I love you, too," Tempestt smiled. "But for real, Sanaa," Tempestt continued. "You deserve more than what your mom thought of you."

Slowly, Sanaa's hands fell from her head. She rested both hands palm down on the counter and avoided looking at Tempestt. Sanaa didn't like what Tempestt said. She had a pit in her stomach that grew and churned incessantly. Tempestt watched as Sanaa's eyes traveled to the window across the kitchen. Sanaa's eyes reflected what her mouth didn't say. Sanaa felt choked up, as though the anger Tempestt described, welled up in Sanaa's soul making its way to her throat. Batting her eyes quickly, Sanaa stretched them as wide as they could go, and then turned her attention back to Tempestt.

"Bitch, I am not crying this morning. I'm drinking, so stop it, okay?"

"No, you're eating," Tempestt corrected. "Let's put something on your stomach before you get sick."

"Pecan pancakes?" Sanaa asked, regaining her composure.

"Pecan pancakes."

Chapter Six

TWO WEEKS LATER

"Sanaa," the voice on the other end crooned.

Sanaa sighed, and her shoulders rose and then fell as his melodic voice washed over her. Sanaa would like to deny it, but she thought about him every day since their encounter.

"Kingston, how are you?" Sanaa tried to sound pleasant but indifferent.

"It's good to hear your voice again," Kingston replied.

"Business going well," Sanaa inquired, leaning to her strength.

"It is, but that's not why I called," Kingston answered.

"No?"

"No," he smiled. "I am back in town for a few days, and I was hoping to see you?"

"Really," Sanaa asked. "Why is that?"

"I think we have some unfinished business," Kington suggested.

"But you said business was going well, Mr. Wells," Sanaa taunted. "Is that not the case?"

"Forgive me for being unclear, Sanaa," Kingston replied. "Wells Woods business is going fine. Wells Woods business with Pinnacle is going fine," Kingston continued. "I'm speaking of unfinished business between Sanaa Chase and Kingston Wells."

"Uhn, between you and me," Sanaa sighed.

"Yes," Kingston replied. "I want to see you."

"I'm not sure why," Sanaa answered, her truest feelings coming to the surface.

Kingston felt it. He remembered the look on Sanaa's face when they last parted. He tried to explain why, but maybe she didn't understand or appreciate it. Kingston was determined to make it up to her.

"Because, Sanaa, I like you," Kingston admitted. "I need to see you."

Sanaa fell quiet, contemplating what her next move should be. Kingston was like an itch she hadn't been able to scratch. She could forget about him and move on to the next nameless man. But something about Kingston stuck in her craw. She didn't like to leave things unfinished. Sanaa refused to be bested. Kingston wasn't sure what to make of the silence on the other end of the line. She could reject him outright. Kingston hoped she wouldn't. He couldn't stop thinking about Sanaa, fantasizing about spending time with her; the inadvertent wrinkle in her nose every time she laughed; the sultry in her eyes when she didn't intend it to be there. Sanaa was the best of everything Kingston desired. She was bright, brilliant, beautiful and elusive. Kingston needed Sanaa to know how he felt about her. He could only do that if she gave him another chance.

Sanaa could be petty, revisiting the rejection she felt from Kingston. Or, Sanaa could use a second meeting as a chance to prove that she was right about Kingston the first time. A devilish smile eased across Sanaa's lips as she made her decision.

"When?"

Two days later

"LEAVING EARLY TODAY, MS. CHASE," CHAUNCEY ASKED AS Sanaa passed her desk.

"Are you checking for me, Chauncey," Sanaa quipped.

"Oh, no," Chauncey corrected. "I didn't mean to. I just wanted to get the last report to you before you left."

"Yes," Sanaa sang. "I am leaving for the day. Send the report to my personal email. And if you need me, I'll be available by phone."

"Good evening, Ms. Chase," Chauncey smiled apologetically.

"Let's hope so," Sanaa winked.

Sanaa traipsed her way to the elevator and made her way to the underground garage. The heels of her shoes clicked rhythmically against the concrete as Sanaa strutted to her car. Sanaa eased into the seat of her BMW 750 and closed the door. Turning on the ignition, Sanaa's Bluetooth connection came alive. Almost immediately, the phone rang.

"Are you psychic," Sanaa asked backing out of the parking space.

"Maybe," Tempestt laughed. "So, tonight's the night, huh?"

"Yes, it is," Sanaa smiled, putting the car in drive and escaping the darkness of the garage. "Yes, it is."

"I don't like the way that sounds, Sanaa," Tempestt cautioned. "You promised you would think about what I said, Sanaa."

"I did, bestie," Sanaa answered.

"And you concluded what may I ask?"

"That I gotta do what I gotta do."

"Really Sanaa? Is that what you decided?" Tempestt questioned.

"T, I can't be you. All I can be is me," Sanaa replied, navigating the BMW onto the expressway.

"That's all I'm asking, Sanaa, is that you be the real you; not the one you've been hiding behind all these years."

Sanaa was in no mood for another heavy conversation. She didn't want to hear anything that would make her think past what she'd already decided.

"Sorry Tempestt, that's my other line."

"Liar," Tempestt chuffed.

"Love you," Sanaa chimed, quickly disconnecting the line.

"Love you, too," Tempestt said into the dial tone.

This time things would be different. This time, Sanaa would be in absolute control. She would have it no other way.

KINGSTON WAS ANXIOUS TO SEE SANAA, SO MUCH SO THAT HE was early; earlier than the fifteen minutes that made him on time. Still, he didn't want to appear too anxious to Sanaa. He could lose cool points for that and Kingston felt like he was already operating at a deficit. So, he would wait, more than the fifteen minutes.

Sanaa did a final check to make sure everything was as it should be; from the food, she had catered into the brandy for after dinner. The music was set to Sanaa's favorite playlist; old school R&B with a few sexy love songs to heighten the mood. Sanaa knew that Kingston was a stickler for time. Sanaa slid on her dress; loose fitting while still flattering, sheer for enticement and a not so gentle reminder and easy access.

Sanaa wasn't the least bit surprised when the doorbell rang. she smiled as she looked at the clock on the wall.

"Right on time," Sanaa mumbled as she made it to the front door.

"Good evening, Sanaa," Kingston strummed.

"Hey Kingston," Sanaa purred opening the door. Her eyes moved slowly, taking in the fullness of Kingston's fine ass frame, all six foot five of it. Kingston's sexy was very easy on the eyes, and Sanaa's jewel thumped in reply. Sanaa took a slight step aside only enough for Kingston to slide by ensuring that she made full body contact as he entered. The smile on Sanaa's face had been devilish before; but as Kingston looked down, his brooding eyes drinking in her essence, Sanaa flushed from the cosmic nature of his touch. Her puss thumped again. She had to have him. What Sanaa tried to shut out was the surge in her heart, the aftermath of Kingston's contact. She would quiet that part of her before the night was over. Sanaa couldn't afford to let her heart get in the way.

"You have a very nice place, Sanaa," Kingston replied, as he unbuttoned his single breast jacket and waited for Sanaa to officially lead him in.

"Thank you, Kingston," Sanaa answered, stepping in front of him so he could follow. Kingston's eyes were naturally drawn to Sanaa's titillating stroll. He momentarily lost all interest in his surroundings and focused solely on the beauty that was before him. But Kingston didn't forget to be a gentleman as the two entered the dining room. He pulled out Sanaa's chair and made sure she was adjusted before he took the seat across from her.

The candlelit dinner, the soft music in the background, and the wine were the perfect backdrop to Kingston and Sanaa reconnecting. With snifters of brandy in hand, Sanaa and Kingston relocated to the living room couch after dinner.

"So, did you enjoy the meal, Kingston," Sanaa flirted.

"It was perfection," Kingston smiled. "Just like you."

"Hmm," Sanaa hummed. "Flattery can get you everywhere."

Lifting slightly from the couch, Sanaa moved closer to Kingston, gently taking the snifter from his hand and sitting it on the sofa table.

"And I do mean everywhere," Sanaa meowed. She locked into Kingston's eyes as she corded her arms around his neck. Sanaa was tired of playing nice. She'd set the trap, and now it was time to devour her prey, finally confirming everything she knew to be true about men, Kingston included. Sanaa's lips rested a mere whisper away from Kingston's mouth.

"Say it again, Kingston," Sanaa whispered.

"What? That you're perfection?"

"Yes, that's it," Sanaa moaned. The first kiss pressed to Kingston's lips was as sweet as it was sensual. Kingston was a man's man, and the feel of Sanaa against his flesh was enough to make his nature rise. Before kissing him again, Sanaa trailed the tip of her tongue across his bottom lip and then pulled his lip into her mouth, sucking it as much as caressing it. Kingston couldn't speak. Sanaa didn't need him to. The moan that escaped his lips was all she needed. Without missing a beat, Sanaa hiked up her dress, mounting Kingston's lap. Her luscious mouth never left contact with his as she pulled his lips into hers, kissing them tenderly and then moaning back as she felt the press of Kingston's manhood against her wanton mound.

"That's right, Kingston, everywhere," Sanaa purred as she pressed hard against his growing shaft; her pert nipples moving against his chest as her tongue explored the wonders of Kingston's mouth.

"Babe, wait," Kingston moaned. "Not like this."

Sanaa heard him, but she was determined to have what she wanted. She refused to be rejected again. Sanaa dropped one arm from around Kingston's neck, moving her hand down the length of him and resting between her thighs. She stroked the thickness of Kingston's manhood, feeling his masculinity respond to her feminine touch.

Kingston moaned again; bis body defying his mind. Sanaa had Kingston just where she wanted him. He was, just a man, after all.

"Sanaa, babe," Kingston started again. He reached for her hand and quieted her stroke. Leaning back just enough, Kingston pulled his mouth out of reach. Sanaa was forced to look at him.

"Not like this," Kingston reasoned maintaining a gaze Sanaa didn't intend.

"Fuck!" Sanaa hissed, pushing against Kingston's chest and lifting herself from him. She flopped back on her side of the couch, frustrated as hell.

"Sanaa, babe, it's not what you think," Kingston offered, reaching his arm around the back of the couch to connect with her. But Sanaa wasn't having that kind of contact. Pushing his hand away, Sanaa bounded from the couch, standing to her feet and folding her arms across her chest. Kingston didn't wait to move. He got up from the couch too, approaching Sanaa.

"It's not what you think, babe," Kinston repeated.

"I don't understand," Sanaa said, as much to herself as to Kingston. Her back was still turned to him. Sanaa felt Kingston's presence close in on her without touching her.

"What don't you understand," Kingston whispered.

She felt the warmth of his breath near her ear which only served to frustrate Sanaa even more.

"What you want from me!" Sanaa fussed, spinning on her naked heels and coming face to face with him. "You said I was perfect. You said you wanted to be with me. What the hell, Kingston."

"All of those things are true, Sanaa. I do think you are perfect just as you are. You are more than desirable, and I do want you," Kingston offered attempting to be reassuring. He took a small step forward, taking a chance.

Then why don't you want me?"

Sanaa didn't intend for her voice to crack. She was angry and confused and hurt and frustrated, but she never intended to sound weak. That was heart shit, and Sanaa wasn't for it. She held her jaw firm and her arms tight, creating a physical barrier between herself and what she had hoped would be her next conquest.

"That's just it, Sanaa, I do," Kingston insisted, bravely, placing his hands on Sanaa's folded arms and encroaching upon the space she held protectively for herself. "Don't misunderstand, I am a man, a real man, and you Sanaa, are a beautiful woman. So, the issue is not whether I want you, because I do, Sanaa. I want you more than you can imagine. It's how I want you."

She didn't want to, but a part of Sanaa heard what Kington said, and it pricked her in a way she definitely hadn't anticipated. Still, she was frustrated by him.

"Does it make a difference," she snided.

"Yes, it does," Kingston affirmed. "It makes a big difference to me." He was no longer willing to be blocked from her and with their eyes locked in a dangerous tango, Kingston unfolded Sanaa's hands, despite her resistance. When she averted her eyes from him, her brow wrinkled and her eyes tight, Kingston took his thumb and rubbed them against her furrows and along the side of her face, gently easing the tension from her eyes. "And I think there's a part of you that knows it makes a difference, too."

"I don't give a damn about that," Sanaa protested. Kingston watched her, trying to bring defiance back into her eyes.

"Really," Kingston asked, taking the curve of her jaw into his hands.

"Really," Sanaa protested.

"Then why are you so mad, beloved?"

The magic voice that soothed her and made her panties wet infuriated Sanaa yet weakened her resolve. Everything Tempestt said to her flooded Sanaa's memory; barging into a space where it was unwanted.

"I only get mad when it matters," Sanaa hissed between clenched teeth. And then Sanaa heard what she said, desperately wanting to take it back. But it was too late. Kingston heard it, too. The enticing smile on his lips said so.

"It matters," Kingston repeated. "It matters, you matter, Sanaa, and I'm going to prove it to you."

She wanted to blow Kingston off. Sanaa wanted to tell him to go to hell so she could move on with her life and forget all about him. But somehow, looking into his depthless eyes and feeling the strength of his soul in Kingston's fingertips, she just couldn't. Sanaa closed her eyes trying to settle the unsettled feeling that moved through her. It felt like the walls she so carefully constructed around her heart were shaking from their very foundation.

When she opened her eyes, Kingston was there; he was right there daring Sanaa to think differently. And when Kingston called her to him, with his eyes and then the fullness of his lips, the decision was made for her.

Chapter Seven

"*W*ill that be all for today," Sanaa's assistant Chauncey asked. The rest of the offices on Sanaa's floor were already darkened as it was well past closing hours.

"Yes," Sanaa answered. "Just don't forget to courier that last contract for the Dalton Group. I want them to have it first thing tomorrow morning.

"Absolutely, Ms. Chase," Chauncey replied. "Have a good evening."

Sanaa had already turned her attention back to the computer monitor even before Chauncey closed the office door. She was intensely watching the stock market, both the United States and international, tracking her clients' progressions and shortfalls in preparation for the next business quarter. Here of late, Sanaa had been super-focused on her work. It wasn't uncommon for Ms. Chase to be the first to arrive at the Pinnacle Group in the morning and the last one to leave at night. Landing the Wells Woods contract was a huge deal for Sanaa. When lead partner Matthew Lawrence acknowledged Sanaa in a company meeting attended by all the partners and several members of the board, Sanaa felt the dirty looks shot in her direction from a few of the old cronie brokers in her office. Some of the same men who approached the Wells Group before and failed to secure the contract were the very one's saltily congratulating Ms. Chase.

She wasn't a part of the old boy's network translation; the old white boys' network and Sanaa had no desire to be. For many of them, they were fine with Sanaa being at Pinnacle, filling the minority quota so they could check off the box that said their company was diverse. They just never wanted Sanaa or any other person of color to upstage them. The fact that she was a woman added insult to injury.

However, none of that was new to Sanaa. She knew going into the brokering arena that she would not be readily reflected in the people around her. Sanaa was determined to keep landing big deals, kicking asses and taking names. She was built for it. Sanaa had her mind on her money and her money on her mind as she continued to track the Dow Jones Industrial Average, Nasdaq and the S&P 500. When Sanaa's cell phone vibrated, she checked the screen deciding whether to answer or not.

On the other end of the line, Tempestt waited for Sanaa to answer. After the third ring Tempestt started to disconnect. She refused to be sent to voicemail.

"Hey girl, what's up," Sanaa asked, putting the phone on speaker so she could keep working on her report.

"I'm checking on you to see how things went with Kingston," Tempestt replied.

"I'm still at work, Temp," Sanaa replied dismissively of the comment.

Since when has that stopped us from having a conversation," Tempestt challenged.

"Since you want to talk about some shit that I don't," Sanaa clapped back.

"Was it really that bad, Sanaa," Tempestt asked, hearing the disdain in her friend's voice.

"Yep," Sanaa quipped.

"You want to get a nightcap and talk about it," Tempestt suggested. She recalled the conversation she and Sanaa had just the other day and how perplexed and frustrated Sanaa was about the situation with Kingston.

"We can get a drink," Sanaa answered, "but we'll be talking about something else."

"Oh," Tempestt paused. "So, you really don't want to talk about Kingston."

"Now you're getting it," Sanaa snided. "But seriously Tempestt, I have about one more hour on this report, and I have to get this done. If you want to have that drink, meet me at my place after that. I don't want to go to a bar. I want to take my bra off and relax in my own space."

See you then, girl," Tempestt agreed. Xavier would be working late this evening. He recently decided to expand Masquerade, and the expansion required additional time. Tempestt didn't mind though. She was fully supportive of Xavier and his business ventures.

Sanaa immediately returned to the report she was working on after disconnecting the phone. Focusing on work minimized the amount of time she had to focus on other things, like men; like Kingston. She didn't want to think about Kingston Wells outside of the confines of their business relationship. It was easier that way. Had Sanaa had any notions that things would turn out the way they did, maybe she would have passed on the Wells deal. But Kingston was as unpredictable as the market could be. She never thought in a million years he would want more than what she willingly offered. That had never happened before, and she still didn't know what to do with it. Wells Woods International; that was her focus, not Kingston Wells III.

Sanaa did her best to be a woman of her word especially when it came to Tempestt. She could have easily worked for much longer, but she promised Tempestt she would keep it to an hour and so she did. Lifting from her executive chair, Sanaa made sure that her computer was locked before sashaying across the office and down the hall towards the elevator. It didn't take long for the boxed car to arrive and even less time for the elevator to descend to the first floor.

"Good evening, Ms. Chase."

"Hey there Mr. Stanford," Sanaa called out. Mr. Cleophus Stanford was one of the night watchmen who secured the Pinnacle Building. He had been with the company for many years and always watched out for Sanaa; even when she insisted there was no need for the security. "How's the wife and grandboy," Sanaa asked as her stilettos clicked across the marble lobby floor.

"Everybody's doing really well," Mr. Stanford replied as he padded in Sanaa's direction. "Another late night I see?"

"Yes," Sanaa smiled. "Another late night."

"Now you didn't ask for any advice from an old man like me, but that doesn't mean I'm not going to give it to you."

"I couldn't stop you if I tried, Mr. Cleophus, so go ahead and lay it on me," Sanaa laughed.

"I know you are a career woman and you are working towards a thing."

"Uhn hun," Sanaa agreed.

"But don't work so much that you don't leave space in your life for love."

Sanaa could only smile. It felt like a universal conspiracy that even the security guard was working against her.

"I hear you Mr. Cleophus," Sanaa smiled.

"But are you listening," Mr. Stanford insisted.

"Mmhmm," Sanaa quipped. Mr. Cleophus shook his head all the while maintaining a pleasant smile. But he was a smart man and knew when to let it go. His wife, Viola, taught him that.

"Now, did you drive in or do you need to wait for a car?"

"I drove in tonight, Mr. Stanford," Sanaa replied.

"Well, let me walk you to your car," Mr. Stanford replied. "And before you tell me I don't have to; I'm going to anyway."

I already know," Sanaa smiled. "Are you this stubborn with the Misses," Sanaa asked as Mr. Stanford held the door open for her to pass through.

"Of course not," Mr. Stanford laughed. "If I had, the wife and I wouldn't be celebrating forty-seven years together, now would we?"

"Probably not," Sanaa smiled. "Well, even though I fuss, you know I appreciate you," Sanaa offered as they approached her car.

"I do," he replied. She hit the locks on the key fob and unlocked the car doors. Mr. Stanford was right there opening her door and waiting until she got seated.

"You be safe now, Ms. Chase, you hear?"

"Yes sir, Mr. Stanford, and I will see you tomorrow."

Cleophus closed the door and took a step back as Sanaa started the engine. Dutifully, he waited until all he could see of Ms. Chase were the red lights from the back of her car. Sanaa was on automatic pilot as she drove home. She didn't think about the turns she made in the car of the names of the streets she traveled down. She'd driven that route plenty of times that outside of the random driver who drove too slowly in front of her, Sanaa didn't think, she just drove. What she did think about was Mr. Stanford. He had been married to the same woman for forty-seven years. That was Sanaa's entire lifetime plus a decade and some change. How could anyone be with one person for that long? Sanaa had been with her family her whole life, but that didn't mean she wanted to be around them constantly. That's why she moved out no sooner than she turned eighteen.

Sounds like restriction to me, Sanaa thought to herself. But that was enough speculation about things that made no sense. Sanaa called for Siri to turn on her playlist to drown out her thoughts. Anthony Hamilton, Keith Sweat, a little Beyoncé and Destiny's Child sped up the ride home. Sanaa wasn't surprised to see Tempestt's car in front of her place.

"How long have you been sitting here," Sanaa said after parking her car.

"Just a few minutes," Tempestt replied. Things at the High Museum where Tempestt worked had been slow recently. Although the museum received incredible private donations, because it was a public facility and received federal dollars, the recent government shutdown had a deleterious impact on the High Museum. They actually had to close their doors for a portion of the shutdown and visitation hadn't quite returned since the shutdown was over. Tempestt, as curator, spent a great deal of her time contemplating how to increase interest in the museum once again. Tempestt could look for inspiration anywhere, even in front of her best friend's house.

The two women padded up the driveway and through the garage to the kitchen door. Once they were inside, Sanaa hit the button to activate the garage door to close.

"So, how was work," Tempestt sang, settling in on the barstool by the kitchen island.

"You don't care about that," Sanaa replied, kicking off her shoes and sitting them by the kitchen door. She would take them to her bedroom closet later, but for now, the shoes would stay.

"I'm trying to start this conversation from a safe place," Tempestt sighed. "Considering how you dissed me on the phone."

"I did no such thing," Sanaa scoffed. Sanaa walked across the kitchen to the wine cabinet.

"Is that what we're drinking," Tempestt asked with a raised brow.

"Oh," Sanaa smiled. "You want a drink drink!"

"Yes, girl, a drinkity drink," Tempestt laughed. She did have ulterior motives in her request for something stronger than a glass of wine. When Sanaa drank, just like with most people, her inhibitions would be lowered, and Sanaa would be more likely to open up about her date with Kingston. That's the real reason Tempestt was there, right? Sanaa must have been okay with drinking something stronger because she wasted no time going to the refrigerator to cold tequila and limes and reaching in the pantry for the salt.

"Do you need a water back or can you hang," Sanaa teased.

"You're funny," Tempestt smiled. "So cute so funny."

Tempestt got up from the barstool and helped Sanaa with the glasses and slicing the limes.

"Do we really have to drink first to talk about Mr. Wells," Tempestt asked without making eye contact with Sanaa. The women stood shoulder to shoulder at the kitchen counter, Tempestt cutting limes and Sanaa rinsing the shot glasses.

"How's Xavier," Sanaa smiled turning in Tempestt's direction.

"He's fine," Tempestt replied. "Was it really that bad?"

"It was and yes, if you are going to make me tell you what happened, then I need a drink or two or three."

"Fine," Tempestt answered, placing a lime wedge on the rims of each of the glasses. Sanaa cracked the seal on the tequila and poured two shots. Both Tempestt and Sanaa poured salt on the backs of their hands and then licked the salt. Lifting their limes and taking a suck, the two picked up the shot glasses.

"Click, click, boom," the girls chorused with two taps of the shot glasses on the counter and a toast in the air before downing the shots in a single gulp.

"Whew, the burn," Tempestt hissed.

"The good kind," Sanaa replied as she poured another shot. "Lick, suck, chuck, baby!" And they did, downing a second a third shot in quick succession.

"Mmm, mmm, mmm," Sanaa groaned, sitting her glass on the counter.

Tempestt held onto the counter as she sat down.

"Before I am too drunk to care, tell me what happened."

Leaning her back against the sink, Sanaa contemplated pouring another shot.

"It was awful, in the worst kind of way awful," Sanaa began as she folded her arms across her ample chest.

"What do you mean? What did he do? Tempestt asked.

"See that's the part that you didn't get before and apparently don't understand now," Sanaa huffed. "It's what he didn't do that's the problem. I had the perfect set up, good food, good drink, a sexy ass outfit, the right music, all of this and his ass turned me down cold."

"Yikes."

"Exactly," Sanaa sighed. "Yikes is right! What full-blooded Alpha male is going to turn this down? I swear, I think something's wrong with him."

"What did he say, though?"

"Oh, all the right bullshit that would probably make another woman swoon, but it just pissed me the hell off. Cause I ain't with the shits. I ain't trying to hear how you want me, but you want me in a special way bullshit."

That's what he said?"

"Does it matter? I mean, at the end of the day does any of that shit matter?"

"Yes, it does," Tempestt replied.

"And that's the biggest damn problem," Sanaa huffed. "Listening to his ass had me thinking that maybe he had a point? Like, for a minute, I was really starting to feel that, I want you for more than just your body. I want to get to know you, blah, blah, blah," Sanaa complained. "Me, Sanaa motherfuckin' Chase, almost fell for the okey-doke."

Tempestt smiled, but she didn't allow the smile to remain on her lips because Sanaa looked at her seeking confirmation that Sanaa was right.

"That is kind of swoon-worthy," Tempestt whispered.

"See there," Sanaa shook her head, "you are too far gone. I need me a truly single friend who's trying to live her best carefree life like me. Huh, you might as well be married up already cause you boo'd up."

"Oh, is that how we're getting down? You trying to replace me with someone who won't ever know you as I know you so they will believe the bullshit you putting down and won't challenge you on said bullshit?" Tempestt countered.

"Don't take that tone with me," Sanaa chuckled feeling all the side eye and neckroll in Tempestt's voice.

"Tuh," Tempestt scoffed.

"What I need to do is go to Masquerade and get some things worked out since Kingston trying to play all Prince Charming and shit."

"Maybe you don't deserve a Prince Charming," Tempestt mused.

"Excuse me?"

"You heard me, Sanaa," Tempestt asserted. "Maybe you don't deserve a Prince Charming."

"Whatever, Temp. I don't want a Prince Charming," Sanaa insisted."

"When Xavier and I got together, were you happy for me? I mean, genuinely happy for me? Or, did you think I was a damn fool? You know, since we talking about replacements and friendships and stuff."

"Don't try me, Tempestt."

"No, for real though, Sanaa. Answer the questions. Let's take them one at a time, so we are both clear, m'kay?" Tempestt didn't wait for a response before launching into the questions.

"Were you happy for me when Xavier and I got together? You know I was," Sanaa scoffed.

"Why?"

"That's a stupid question."

"No, it's really not," Tempestt replied. "So, answer it."

"Because, Tempestt," Sanaa began. "That's what you wanted."

"Okay, why do you think I wanted it?"

"Cause," Sanaa rolled her eyes, "you like that love type of shit."

"And you don't?"

The clapback was quick and dirty. If Sanaa answered in the same way, fast with no hesitation, then she would say something that even in thinking about it sounded dumb.

"I like that love type of shit for people who like that love type of shit," Sanaa answered.

"Such a non-starter, but okay, for the sake of argument, let's go with that," Tempestt replied. "At one point you said that you almost fell for Kingston wanting to get to know you in the right way. Why do you think that is?"

"Weak," Sanaa answered.

"Do you think I'm weak?"

"I thought we were talking about me," Sanaa sassed.

"We are," Tempestt replied. "Still, answer the question."

"Do I think you're weak," Sanaa repeated."

"Mmhmm," Tempestt asserted. "Do you think I'm weak?"

"We aren't the same, Tempestt," Sanaa suggested. "That's why we get along so well," Sanaa said offering a fake toothy smile.

"That may be true, but a few moments ago you wanted to replace me with, who, someone who thinks like you?"

Tempestt continued. "That was rhetorical so don't bother answering. This is my point. Most people do not have completely dichotomous thoughts about the same subject. However, you seem to. For example, if a man is nice to you and you like it, you're weak. In the same breath, if a man is nice to me and I like it, I'm not weak. And if you want to keep riding with that tired argument that we're two different people, that's cool. I can go with that," Tempestt sighed. "But the bigger question, the one I've been leading up to that you keep trying to derail because you know it's coming, is why does it make you weak? Why not Prince Charming?"

"Prince Charming isn't real though; you know that, right?" Sanaa countered.

Tempestt's eyes narrowed.

"Fine," Sanaa whined, copping to another attempt at derailing the real conversation. "I need another shot."

"Deflection," Tempestt countered, snatching up the tequila and placing it behind her.

"Falling for his kindness makes me weak because it can't last. I'm just trying to skip over all the emotional stuff because, at the end of the day, kindness doesn't last. Prince Charming isn't real, and kindness doesn't last. Instead of going through all the rigmarole of being nice to me so you can get in my panties and take from me because that's all you really want, I take the offensive; shut down the emotions, give the panties drawers to who I want to, the way I want to, when I want to, and then move the fuck on, leaving them to deal with whatever feelings and emotions they have." Sanaa shrugged her shoulders. "Kindness doesn't last, Tempestt; it just doesn't."

"Does that only apply to you? The men you encounter or am I setting myself up for the okey doke, too? Cause if it's all men, and not just you, then how the hell could you be genuinely happy for me?"

Silence.

Nothing.

Sanaa had no comeback.

"Kingston had the unmitigated gall to suggest that I should think differently," Sanaa offered after a few tense moments trying to sound as irritated as she did before.

"Nah, why bother?" Tempestt sighed, crossing her legs and folding her arms.

"I would agree with you, but I know you're trying to be funny."

"Not in the least," Tempestt answered. "Just trying to be a good bestie."

"So, you're going to agree with everything I say now, huh?"

"Isn't that what you want, Sanaa? Because even somewhat drunk I know we have had the same conversations over and over ad nauseum. You don't listen you think you're right, got everything under control, and happy as hell and clearly, you're smarter stronger, and more together than anyone else, so why bother?"

"You're the one who wanted to talk, remember?"

"Yeah, I did," Tempestt agreed, "hoping that you would give the ole boy a chance. But since you don't intend to, then leave him alone. Don't ruin him for someone else."

Chapter Eight

TWO WEEKS LATER

*K*ingston Wells stood looking out of the large picture window of his Colorado home. Just beyond the three acres of manicured land that comprised his front yard, lay acre upon acre of heavily wooded mountainous terrain that remained unspoiled by human hands. Kingston stood in front of the window a lot. It was one of the reasons he had the house built facing the direction it was because of the amazing views. From Kingston's vantage point he could see how big the sky was, how bright the stars could be, how dark and heavy the clouds looked when there was a storm brewing and how peaceful the atmosphere was when it snowed. Although Wells Woods International had corporate offices in Denver as well as Atlanta every chance Kingston got, he stayed at his Colorado home. He loved it there because of the remoteness, because of the serenity and the occasional surprise of a deer or an elk meandering across his front yard. From his home office, Kingston coordinated with the corporate sites, conducted teleconferences, and handled business meetings virtually. But the meeting with Ms. Chase and the Pinnacle Group? That meeting required his presence. And ever since that meeting, he couldn't keep his mind off Sanaa.

Kingston shifted as he heard a rhythmic noise behind him the paws of his jet black, Great Dane, Zeus, padding softly across the Brazilian hardwood floors.

"Hey, big boy," Kingston greeted as Zeus came to rest near him. Zeus loved the picture window too, especially when furry creatures that he wanted to chase happened by.

Since their last date, Kingston replayed that evening multiple times in his head. Kingston was hopeful that Sanaa would give him a chance; a real chance to court her and get to know her and woo her because that's what she deserved is a man who wanted to woo her. There was a moment that night when they were together, that Kingston felt he saw past Sanaa's quick wit and sexy charm and got a glimpse of the person Sanaa really was. Just beyond the beauty of her eyes, Kingston saw pain. She tried to cloak it and turn away when she felt he looked too deeply into her, but that hadn't stopped Kingston from seeing. Yet, Kingston didn't want to be presumptuous when it came to Sanaa. He didn't want to assume anything about what he saw. What Kingston wanted was for Sanaa to get comfortable enough with him that she would speak to her own situation; that she clarify what he actually saw and what that meant for Sanaa.

Kingston didn't want to push. However, there was a part of Kingston that felt like staying away too long would undermine what he was trying to establish with Sanaa. Too much time to second guess, and counter, and contemplate and speculate would create opportunities for doubt; doubt about thinking differently.

"Zeus, should I call her?" Kingston asked of his four-legged friend.

Zeus barked vigorously.

"Good answer, big guy," Kingston laughed. "Good answer."

Kingston strolled to the oversized leather chair that sat at the optimal juxtaposition to the window. Sitting down, he reached over to the side table and picked up his cell phone. Sometimes because of his location, cell service could be spotty. However, because of the need to be connected particularly for business, Kingston paid for every upgrade to ensure that he could reach who he needed to reach wherever they were; in this case Sanaa Chase. Kingston checked his watch being mindful of the time difference. Atlanta was two hours behind Colorado. It was Wednesday, at nine o'clock Kingston's time, eleven o'clock Sanaa's. Unlocking his phone, Kingston speed dialed Sanaa's number. Sanaa was in her office, as usual, sending a fax. She'd let Chauncey go home an hour or so before, so Sanaa was handling her own secretarial duties. The building was quiet. She liked it that way. When her phone rang, the ringtone echoed through the emptied office space.

"Coming," Sanaa sighed as the trotted back to her desk in the four-inch pumps she wore. "Coming, coming, coming," Sanaa fussed as the phone rang again.

Reaching her desk, Sanaa checked the caller ID. It was Kingston. Sanaa sighed heavily and sat down in her chair in much the same way. To answer or not to answer? That was the million-dollar question. Sanaa resented Kingston for his suggestion that somehow her thought processes were flawed. Still, she found herself attracted to him; his desire to prove himself different than the rest. To answer or not to answer? She still hadn't decided when the phone stopped ringing; the automated voicemail system deciding for her. Leaning back in her chair, Sanaa waited to see if Kingston would leave a voicemail.

Why was her heart beating so," Sanaa considered, feeling the thumping in her chest. *You ran to the phone girl*, Sanaa self-chastised. And then she heard his voice, completely filling up the empty space.

"Hey gorgeous," Kingston's sexy baritone voice crooned. "I hope this message finds you well."

There was an elongated pause Sanaa hadn't anticipated.

She leaned forward, resting her elbows on the table wondering if Kingston had more to say.

"I was just thinking about you, so I thought I'd call. Talk soon."

"Talk soon," Sanaa repeated. "Presumptuous much?"

Ignoring the increased thump in her chest, and the pull on her yoni, Sanaa popped her lips and got up from the chair. She returned to the fax machine, walking, holding her thighs much more tightly together. On the other end of the line, Kingston was a little disappointed when Sanaa didn't pick up. He really did want to hear her voice, connect with her. Maybe she would call ack, Kingston wasn't sure. Maybe he needed to have something much more intelligent to say the next time he called.

Talk soon.

Why was that two-word commentary bothering Sanaa so much?

Those two words ran across her mind as she walked back from the fax machine, as she sat down in her office chair, as she monitored the stock report, as she eventually got into the elevator and rode it to the first floor. Even as Mr. Cleophus gave her an update about his precarious grandson and the shenanigans they'd gotten into since the last time she and Mr. Stanford spoke, Sanaa was distracted by Kingston's last two words. It was promissory and mighty damn assumptive.

"That's all he wants to do is talk," Sanaa grumbled as she climbed into her car after another long night at the office. Sanaa was bothered; she wasn't tired. Sanaa had a hankering that needed to be filled. And since Kingston clearly hadn't been up to the challenge, Sanaa knew exactly where to find someone who would. A stealthy smile eased across her lips.

She knew just where to go. Sanaa didn't need a navigational system to get to her destination. Within minutes, Sanaa pulled up to VIP at Masquerade. The valet opened her car door and smiled as Sanaa slung her shapely legs over the driver's seat and stepped out. She felt his eyes on her ass as she sashayed toward the front door of the club. Sanaa's smile remained as she paused looked over her shoulder and winked at the valet. Her wink and a smile made that young man's night.

Sanaa stood in front of the door to Masquerade. The intricately carved heavy mahogany wood door with oversized brass handles, standing nearly twelve feet in height would intimidate most people. The two enormous guards flanking the door; their eyes shielded and their faces solemn would be enough to intimidate most people. But not for Sanaa. It was a welcomed sight.

"Password, please," one of the guards asked, turning slightly in Sanaa's direction.

"Please me," she purred in response.

Satisfied with her answer, the same guard reached for the handle and pulled the door open allowing Sanaa's admission. Her eyes had to make an immediate adjustment from the fluoresced darkness of outdoors to the ambient golden light that illuminated the interior. Reaching in her clutch, Sanaa pulled out her VIP membership card, flashing it at the receptionist.

"Good evening, Ms. Chase," the receptionist replied.

"Good evening."

With the press of a button, Sanaa gained entrance to the inner sanctum of Masquerade. She paused at the mirrored door only to check the perfection of her reflection in the mirror. Stepping across the threshold, Sanaa welcomed the familiar crimson light that washed over her body. The ruby red glow was both haunting and disorienting, making any movement mysterious and piquing one's curiosity. Sanaa enjoyed the anonymous others moving around her. She could disappear behind the secrecy of the club while still being herself. Sanaa could be indulgent without judgment or misplaced emotions put upon her by others. Inside Masquerade, Sanaa was free.

There were many destinations within the walls of Masquerade; some public and some ultra-private. Some rooms were just for observation while others were for full participation. Sanaa knew exactly where she wanted to be and took the first step in that direction. As Sanaa moved her olfactory senses were teased with the titillating scents of frankincense and myrrh, the signature olfactory aphrodisiac known in Masquerade. Someone brushed just past her and Sanaa's nose was tickled again with the smell of vanilla and feminine essence. The mystique of it all sent warm waves coursing to Sanaa's core. She turned a corner and passed through another door. The crimson from the main room faded as the new room bathed Sanaa in deep moody purples.

The room consisted of a small stage and several chairs for the audience. Music played through the surround sound system offering lyrical melodies and a deep bass beat. It gave the room a pulse, beating and reverberating like the rhythm of an excitedly pounding heart. Those with exhibitionist tendencies utilized the stage with its low beam spotlights to show off, while those with voyeuristic tendencies had the pleasure of watching along with others who enjoyed a good show just as much. As Sanaa found a seat near the middle of the room, the stage was empty. Much like any performance, there was a call time, and the show in the Purple Haze room would begin at any moment.

Another anonymous other entered the room, shadowy, and sat immediately behind Sanaa. At almost the same time, there was movement on the stage, bodies, circling, teasing, luring before what every audience member knew would be salacious entanglement. The beam of the spotlight found two people on stage; a woman standing freely; a man, bound ankles and wrists to an X shaped bondage board. Sanaa's curiosity was instantly piqued; a woman taking control. It was the mantra for her very own soul. Just seeing the woman standing there scantily clad and looking sexy completely in charge of the tall, darkly handsome man titillated Sanaa's senses. His eyes were on her, inhaling her, watching to see what she would do with him. Whether they knew each other before this moment, whether they had a history together or this was a random encounter, none of that mattered. She was the captor, and he was the prey.

Sanaa's chest rose and fell as she was consumed with anticipation of what was to come.

Talk soon — Kingston's words. Just talk.

She sauntered towards him, never letting her eyes fall from him. Sanaa could see that even as the woman drew nigh to him, his body was already reacting to her approach. His muscled chest lifted and dropped as he breathed in deeper. Sanaa could see the strain of the man's arms against the cuffs, and the rise of the man's dick as the woman got closer. Sanaa crossed her legs to quell the pull she felt from a jewel that had gone untouched, unsatiated for far too long. The woman reached her captured man and stood in front of him, close enough that if he was not bound, he could reach her, grab her, pull the woman to him and ravage her. But he couldn't. He couldn't reach her and the strain against the cuffs, his muscles rippling in his forearms, his pecs flexing in his chest and the long muscles of his thighs tensing and releasing as the woman stood just shy of his throbbing inches.

Sanaa adjusted uncomfortably in her seat as the woman on the stage extended her hands, one to the man's well-toned chest and the other to the base of his thick nine-inch pulsating shaft. The look of pure angst and ecstasy on the man's face sheared a heated core down Sanaa's spine, and she squirmed in her chair again.

"I can help you with that," a deep, throaty voice blew against the back of her neck.

Sanaa's posture lifted bracing and melding from the warmth of the unexpected breath behind her. She didn't turn in that direction, though. Sanaa was busy, completely occupied by the show in front of her, as the woman eradicated the distance between herself and her captor and then lifted her thigh high against his waist so that the voyeurs looking on could see as she guided his thumping cock into her wet folds. When the woman gasped from his directed impaling, others in the room did too, including Sanaa. She squeezed her thighs together as tight as she could get them as her yoni pulsed and vibrated between her legs. Her eyes narrowed, and her mouth fell slightly open as she watched the woman push against the man's swollen member, making it disappear inside her and reappear and then disappear again as she fucked this man standing up. The woman was in complete control and Sanaa's pussy moistened in response. She was the woman, vicariously.

The unknown stranger was still right there behind Sanaa breathing in her space, infringing upon her space.

"Let me help you," he crooned and then kissed the back of Sanaa's neck. It would be so easy to give in to her most base desire; to get what she wanted for this stranger satisfy her own needs and walk away liked she done before. She could take out all her sexual frustration with Kingston on this anonymous stranger and walk away utterly satisfied. She could. He was willing. This man was willing to do what Kingston wanted to talk about later. He kissed her again, tracing his tongue in small centers at the base of Sanaa's neck. The escalation and the pant from her lips urged Sanaa to give in. It would be so easy. Sanaa lifted her head against the press of his probing tongue, and she watched the intense fuck happening right in front of her. The man laced his fingers around the front of Sanaa's neck and trailed hot kisses to her ear.

"Let me," he moaned.

Sanaa's nipples pressed hard against the fabric of her silk

shirt. Her body cried out for a masculine touch. But, not just any touch.

Sanaa uncrossed her legs and stood up, quickly exiting the room. She was still panting from exhilaration and the potential of sweet relief. As she exited Masquerade moving faster going out than she did coming in, Sanaa realized that it wasn't just any relief that she wanted. It wasn't just some anonymous stranger she wanted to give herself to. Sanaa exited Masquerade and stepped into the late-night air. There was a coolness, a crispness without being chilly. Breathing in deeply, Sanaa filled her lungs and then released the air slowly through her pouty lips. She watched as the heat from her mouth met the cool of the air, leaving a trail of mist that faded into nothingness. Breathing new air, not the filtered the purple haze or crimson ambient light, helped clear the cobwebs from her mind. As she waited for the valet to bring her car, the tightness in Sanaa's thighs started to dissipate. The churning in her gut began to subside. The strain of unresolved sexual tension began to release. A stranger would not do, not this time. Some anonymous other is not what would satisfy Sanaa she reluctantly realized.

Talk soon…

As Sanaa climbed into her car, those words danced across her memory. She couldn't even frown behind it; instead, focusing on the sound of Kingston's voice, the soothing timbre that inclined her to him and appeased her in all Sanaa's soft places. As she made her way down the road, Sanaa shook her head in disbelief.

Sanaa wanted Kingston.

It was Kingston she wanted; maybe even for the right reasons.

Chapter Nine

*S*anaa wasn't much of a traditionalist when it came to the art of male-female entanglements. That goes without saying. However, Sanaa was reticent to reach out to Kingston, to return his call even as she sat at her desk the following day staring at her phone, willing it to ring with a call from Mr. Wells. She could call Kingston, say she missed his previous call and was merely responding. That wouldn't be Sanaa making the first move, or any move really. Except, she knew her intention for reaching out was more than that, ergo the problem. For Sanaa, that kind of extension of herself had the potential to reveal her hand. It read as weak. Sanaa shook her head as Tempestt's poignant questions, and challenges to her thought processes played in the background. Sanaa was still salty about that. She knew Tempestt meant well and that Tempestt wanted the best for her. Still, Tempestt could never truly understand what it was like being betrayed by the one person who was supposed to love Sanaa unconditionally; the one person who was supposed to believe Sanaa without question. The pain of that, the hurt from that? Unless a person had been through that level of rejection, they couldn't understand. Just thinking about it made Sanaa's gut churn.

But Sanaa didn't hold it against Tempestt. It just meant that Sanaa would have to take Tempestt's words, lectures, and forthright challenges as a grain of concerned salt. She still loved Tempestt like a sister, though. Sanaa wouldn't dare let Tempestt in on her little situation. Sanaa would keep that to herself; at least for now.

"Excuse me, Ms. Chase?"

"Yes, Chauncey," Sanaa replied to the light knock on her partially opened door.

"You've got a call on line one."

"Thank you, Chauncey," Sanaa answered. She waited until Chauncey exited to react to the news. There was racing in Sanaa's heart that told her one thing. She smiled thinking it was Kingston. It had to be. Why else would her heart be beating so fast and the freshness of new adrenaline pulsing through her veins. Sanaa figured that since Kingston was unable to reach her on the cell phone, he was reaching out to her another way. Sanaa allowed the line to blink another second before answering. She didn't want to appear anxious.

"This is Ms. Chase," Sanaa sang wearing a wickedly sinister smile. She waited to hear that voice that she'd come to know so well.

"Good afternoon, Ms. Chase."

It wasn't who Sanaa expected, and the deflated smile on her face was proof of that.

"How can I help you, Mr. Lawrence?"

It was Sanaa's boss. This was business. Sanaa sat back in her seat and listened to see what Matthew wanted.

"You have a request for a meeting in Colorado. Your flight leaves in two hours."

"Excuse me, what?"

Now Sanaa was sitting up straight in her executive chair.

"You have a request for a meeting, Ms. Chase, a very important meeting with an extremely important client. Be prepared to leave for your flight," Mr. Lawrence advised.

"Understood," Sanaa replied. "But can I at least know who the client is?"

"Absolutely, Ms. Chase," Lawrence answered. "Wells Woods International."

Sanaa's mouth fell open. She had to pull it together though as the silence after Mr. Lawrence's statement started to feel awkward.

"If there's a problem, Ms. Chase, I expect you to handle it. If there is anything Mr. Wells and his multimillion-dollar company need to ensure he remains with us, I expect you to take care of it. I want him happy and content after this meeting, Ms. Chase. Do we understand each other?"

"Absolutely, Mr. Lawrence," Sanaa replied, snapping back into professional mode. "I'll take care of it."

"I expect nothing less. Have a great trip."

Sanaa still held the receiver in her hand as the line disconnected. Slowly, she collapsed into the comfort of her chair. Sanaa didn't know how to feel about what she just heard.

"Chauncey!"

Sanaa didn't bother to use the phone she finally hung up, hard.

She could hear Chauncey scurrying to reply. Chauncey wouldn't be so callous as to yell back.

"Yes, Ms. Chase?" Chauncey replied, slightly winded, or maybe she was breathing hard because she knew something was wrong. For Ms. Chase to break decorum and scream like she just did? There was something wrong.

"I have to go to Colorado unexpectedly. I don't know what the temperature in Colorado is like, but I expect that it's cold; colder than I'm used to." Methodically, Sanaa raised up from leaning so deeply in the chair. Chauncey's eyes were still wide, trying to figure out what the hell was going on and praying that it wasn't because she screwed up in some way.

"So, I need you to go to the mall, Chauncey. First, check the weather, then go to the mall. Use the business platinum card since they are the ones sending me and find me some things that are warm enough to wear in Colorado. Make sure they are hella expensive and don't scrimp. If I am being summoned to a meeting in Colorado in the next two hours, the least I can be is warm."

"Will do Ms. Chase," Chauncey replied both curious and relieved. "Anything else?"

"Yes, Chauncey," Sanaa said as she stood to her feet. Chauncey was still trying to read her. Sanaa's face was flat, but her words spewed from her lips with disdain and heightened emotionality. "Reschedule my afternoon meetings. Push them, make up an excuse if you have to, but push everyone. And meet me at my place in an hour."

The task seemed insurmountable, but Chauncey worked miracles for Ms. Chase before. She would do it again, and with a smile. Chauncey took a deep breath and started calculating her next moves in her head.

"Absolutely, Ms. Chase. I will see you in an hour."

Two hours later

"REFRESHMENT, MA'AM?"

Typically, before an important meeting, Sanaa wouldn't drink. She would reserve that business luxury to after business was handled.

"Bourbon straight, no chaser," Sanaa answered.

The stewardess smiled as she recorded the order and moved to the next patron in first class.

Sanaa tried to relax in the comfort of first class. She couldn't. Sanaa hadn't been able to relax or think clearly since the call from Lawrence. She replayed the conversation, as one-sided as it was repeatedly. Was this all a ploy to get a response? It's not like Kingston called multiple times and she failed to respond. Sanaa sent the man to voicemail one time, and now she had a meeting; a meeting routed through the lead partner in her company kind of meeting.

What the hell!?!?!

That's the only consistent thing Sanaa thought since talking to her boss. When the stewardess doubled back with the drink Sanaa requested, she put up a cautionary hand, downed the dark brown liquor and handed the stewardess an empty glass.

"One more?" The stewardess asked with an understanding grin.

Sanaa checked her watch and calculated the length of the flight.

"Just one more," Sanaa winked. She would pull it together before the plane landed, put on her professional badass pimp-style hat, and handle the meeting like the consummate businesswoman she was. In the meantime, while Sanaa flew hundreds of miles to see the man, who rejected her and challenged Sanaa to think differently, she would stay cool. But after all, business was handled successfully? All bets with Kingston Wells were off.

...summoning me... tuh!

THE AIRPORT IN DENVER COLORADO WAS MUCH SMALLER than the one Sanaa was used to. There was still the hustle and bustle of people coming and going trying to get to their respective destinations, but it wasn't the same. There was something else decidedly different. Even within the confines of the airport, all it took was a glance to the nearest window to see that it was cold as hell. Seeing the whiteness of it all made Sanaa feel the chill even before stepping outside. She nestled the wool scarf Chauncey bought her tightly around her neck and pulled the winter coat more snuggly around her shoulders before taking the first step outdoors. When Chauncey checked the arrangements, there was to be a car waiting for Sanaa. She hoped like hell that was the case because as cold as it looked from inside had nothing on just how frigid the air really was. It was enough to snatch Sanaa's breath away as the first inhale of Denver air chilled her to the bone.

There were only a few people waiting outside the gate, and only one holding up a sign that read Wells Woods. *What do you expect on a Thursday afternoon in cold-ass Colorado*, Sanaa thought to herself as she quickly shuffled in the direction of the driver.

"Ms. Chase," the older gentleman asked.

"Yes," Sanaa answered through teeth threatening to chatter.

"Right this way," the driver replied, taking the small bag and briefcase from Sanaa and ushering her to the car. She climbed in quickly, grateful when the driver closed the door behind her. Sanaa immediately felt the difference in temperature as the chauffeur had the heat on. The Cadillac Escalade SUV was toasty, and Sanaa didn't hesitate to place her chilled hands over the heating vent until they thawed. The driver climbed in and with a swift glance to the rearview mirror, he put the car in gear an pulled out of the parking space. Sanaa had seen snow before; Atlanta snow – pretty, white, dissipating quickly. She even chuckled as her eyes scanned from one side of the vehicle to the other seeing not mere inches but what looked like feet of the white stuff. Just the threat of snow in Atlanta was enough for there to be all out runs on the grocery store; shelves cleared of all the essentials, schools and government offices closed in advance of the first snowflake falling. What in the world did the people in Colorado do when the snow stayed on the ground in huge mounds seemingly all over the place?

Delivery. That's what Sanaa figured as the car moved carefully down the curvy roadway. Although there were areas in Atlanta where green spaces abound, those areas were on the periphery of the city. Looking out of the window, all Sanaa could see was tall trees rising above the mounds of snow beneath, evergreens closer to the ground and comingling with the white stuff and the bluest mid-afternoon sky she'd seen in a long time. Sanaa was astute enough to know that Denver was a thriving metropolis, but the chauffeur-driven SUV didn't appear to be heading in that direction. The truck took on a relatively steep incline. The road remained curvy, but this time the windy roads curved around deeper groves of trees. Reaching in her clutch, Sanaa pulled out a breath mint to freshen up. They weren't in the business district though.

Sanaa's attention was fully drawn to the passenger side window as the vehicle entered an unexpected clearing. In the distance, Sanaa could see an extravagant residence, appropriate for the Colorado mountains, with large picture windows, stonework and a few logs for that rustic touch. The smirk that moved across Sanaa's lips couldn't be missed.

"Excuse me, sir," Sanaa asked getting the driver's attention. "Where are we?"

"The Wells estate, ma'am."

"The meeting is here and not let's say the Colorado headquarters for Wells Woods International?"

"My instructions were to bring you here, ma'am," the driver confirmed.

Sanaa sat back against the leather of the seat. She had been summoned, but why? Sanaa decided she would temporarily reserve judgment. She was curious to see what Kingston was up to. The driver turned the SUV to the right and maneuvered the vehicle down a cobblestone drive to a portico in the front of the estate. Sanaa's eyes tracked towards the front door. When the door opened, a large dog stepped out and stood just outside the door. The driver put the car in park and then came to open Sanaa's door.

"Is that dog going to bite me?" She asked nervously.

"Zeus? He's harmless," a familiar voice replied. Sanaa's eyes traveled to that voice. Her eyes narrowed, and there was a slight uptick to the curve of her lip. Although Sanaa's eyes were enchanted by the look of him. So tall, so regal and amazingly handsome, there was still a tinge of 'what the hell Kingston was up to' that lingered. Sanaa was both intrigued and irritated. She just hadn't decided which was the overriding emotion.

"I'll take it from here, Mike, thanks," Kingston said as he strode towards the SUV. Mike nodded and walked away. Kingston turned to Sanaa. Instantly, his face adjusted to the presence of her form. His eyes took her in with a sweeping glance; pleasantly reminding Kingston of the depth of her eyes, the curve of her scintillating lips, the elegance of her neck and the brown of her beautiful skin. He could see the question in her eye, but that didn't dissuade Kingston in the least.

"Hello, gorgeous."

There was a quip on the tip of Sanaa's tongue. She held it seeing the way Kingston gazed at her. Sanaa felt as though Kingston was literally drinking her in with his eyes, appraising every facet of her; the good and the bad. And yet, he still smiled; not just with his lips. Kingston's gaze was disarming in a way Sanaa refused to acknowledge before. Maybe she hadn't taken the time to assess it because of her hell-bent intentions of taking him. Sanaa saw it this time, undeniably. Kingston extended his hand to Sanaa. Their eyes locked as she accepted. Kingston helped Sanaa out of the truck and closed the door behind her. Kingston's hand found the small of Sanaa's back and gently rested there.

"You have some explaining to do, Mr. Wells," Sanaa insisted with a cheeky smile.

"I know," Kingston drummed. "I'm just glad you're here."

Turning on her heels, Sanaa looked up into Kingston's dark, brooding eyes.

"Did I really have a choice?" her upturned chin and the glint in Sanaa's eyes pricked Kingston's heart. He told her before that he desired her, that he wanted her. Seeing her again was a soul-stirring reminder.

"Hopefully, by the time we're done, you'll forgive this transgression," Kingston replied and then leaned in close to Sanaa's ear. "If you'd still call it that."

The searing heat of Kingston's warm breath against the nakedness of her flesh charred a heated path straight through Sanaa's core momentarily shielding her from the cold existing around her.

"We'll see," Sanaa whispered, pressing into Kingston's lips that still remained there. Kingston inhaled her scent. Even in the cooled air, Sanaa's aura was penetrating and sent a quickening to Kingston's core.

Sanaa's attention was distracted from the strength of Kingston's muscular frame to the click of Zeus' paws as he approached.

"Uhm," Sanaa hummed; her eyes widening as the large beast approached. Instinctively she leaned against Kingston. He felt her body shake against him.

"Zeus, sit," Kingston commanded.

Sanaa watched as the dog immediately responded to his master.

"Now, I'm not one of those dog owners who tells you the dog doesn't bite, and you shouldn't be afraid. Zeus does bite," Kingston replied. Sanaa grabbed Kingston around the waist, uncomforted by his words. "Let me finish," Kingston smiled as he gently kissed Sanaa on the forehead. "He only bites when he is defending his territory, or he or I am under attack. Are you going to attack me, Ms. Chase?"

"No," Sanaa quipped. "Well maybe," she teased.

Kingston smiled widely. "With the intent to hurt me?"

Sanaa hooded her brow and tried to look stern and intense. But the glimmer in her eye was still there. Kingston wrapped both his arms around her waist and pulled Sanaa into him.

"Now, I want you to walk over to Zeus with me. Give him a chance to sniff your scent. He would never hurt you, but I want you to be comfortable around him. If you are not, though, I will put him away,"

"That means I have to trust you," Sanaa mused.

"It does," Kingston crooned. They entangled in another entrancing gaze. This was more than about the dog, and they both knew it. The question in Sanaa's eyes said so. The assurance in Kingston's said the same.

"Okay," Sanaa sighed.

"Yes," Kingston replied. "It is okay to trust me."

Sanaa clutched Kingston's waist and gently nodded her head. This time, she was going against her gut. She wasn't a fan of dogs. Sanaa had never really given herself a chance to be around them. Sanaa knew it was more; and for the second time since meeting Kingston, she was willing to trust where she'd never otherwise trusted. Kingston took his cue and moved them in Zeus' direction. The Great Dane's ears were alert, but his eyes were soft and focused on Kingston.

"That's good, beautiful. Don't be nervous," Kingston encouraged. "He's going to smell you, but it's okay."

"I'm trusting you, Kingston."

Zeus did exactly as Kingston said; lifting on his hind legs and leaning forward, sniffing in Sanaa's direction.

"…oh my god," Sanaa mumbled as Zeus stood to his full height. She noticed that Zeus' tail was wagging. "He's so big!"

"He is," Kingston laughed. "But he's really just a big baby."

Sanaa wasn't as nervous about Zeus as she thought she would be. Trepidatiously, she extended her hand to reach for the canine.

"Oh, my," Sanaa sighed when Zeus leaned in and licked her hand.

"See, beautiful, he likes you," Kingston grinned.

"That's a relief." Sanaa giggled.

"He's got good taste like his daddy," Kingston added.

Zeus turned on his haunches and moved towards the house.

"Uhn, so you like me," Sanaa quipped as they started toward the house.

"Yes," Kingston replied; tapering his stride to match hers. "But you already knew that."

Once they arrived at the door of the estate, Kingston stepped aside and allowed Sanaa to cross the threshold before stepping in behind Sanaa and closing the door. The beauty that Sanaa noted outside of the estate paled in comparison to how striking the residence was on the inside. The hardwood floor that extended from the entryway for as far as Sanaa's eyes could see was like no other floor she'd seen before. There was a subtle shine that reflected the sun's rays while managing to capture some of the brightness that danced off the surface. Sanaa's eyes immediately traveled up to the vault of the high-pitched ceiling. The texture is what drew her eye. The ceiling seemed to wave and bevel with wooden logs reminiscent in color to the hardwood floor. The windows in the home seemed to be endless; large and unobstructed. The views were sweeping and breathtaking even from where Sanaa stood. Although with one look it was clear the furnishings in the home were high-end, none Sanaa could see seemed ostentatious; too over the top screaming money. It all made sense to Sanaa as she meandered down the long hallway a few steps behind Kingston. They're family specialized in timber. The estate would have the absolute finest timber used in the most innovative ways.

Kingston slowed his stroll when the duo approached an office. Sanaa paused and then a slithering smile moved across her luscious lips. Her briefcase was already in the room, like magic.

"Business after all, huh?" Sanaa quipped.

Kingston pivoted to face her.

"I would never lie to you, Sanaa," Kingston strummed. Never."

Kingston stepped to Sanaa, eliminating the distance between them. Inhaling deeply, his olfactory senses were teased with her intoxicating scent. There was a thump in his heart that pounded behind his massive chest. There was a second thump that reminded him of his desire. Easing the chair, Kingston held it until Sanaa was comfortably seated and then took up residence in the chair next to her. She felt something too; the truth of what Kingston said. Sanaa didn't hear it with her ears. She heard it past the barricade surrounding her wounded heart.

"That's good to know," Sanaa replied. "So, Mr. Wells, how can Pinnacle be of service to you?"

Kingston shook his head and laughed. "Touché, Ms. Chase." Kingston reached for a folder and handed it to Sanaa. Her eyes trekked to Kingston before opening the folder. She thought the trip might have been an elaborate ruse. Opening the folder, Sanaa looked at the information that was there, and her curiosity was piqued. Kingston appraised Sanaa as she perused the contents. She got such a stern look on her face when she was in business mode. There was a slight pitch to a single eyebrow and the slightest pout to her lips when the wheels in her beautiful mind turned. Kingston found that look sexy as hell.

"If I'm reading this correctly, you're considering an acquisition?"

"That's right," Kingston replied, drawing himself from his fantasy back to the conversation at hand. "There is a company operating out of Canada that, if we acquire, would open up markets that otherwise would be pretty much off limits to us."

"Are they considering selling," Sanaa asked, reaching in her briefcase and pulling out her computer. It didn't take long for the machine to power up. Sanaa did a search on the company as they continued to talk. They were sitting close enough for each to feel the aura of the other. There was a wave of energy that passed between the two that at times was intense enough almost to be seen. With their hands in close proximity, all one had to do was make a slight reach and their bodies would be connected. The underlying sexual tension was enough that it was undeniable. Sanaa did her best to concentrate on the business at hand. She didn't dare let Kingston know that he had that kind of effect on her. Kingston struggled as well. He knew Sanaa was suspicious of her reason for being there. He pushed himself to focus on the business end of things.

"There are rumors that there is infighting within the executive committee which is causing rumblings throughout the company."

"What's your concern," Sanaa asked hearing hesitation in Kingston's voice.

"Wells Woods has a stellar reputation as an honorable company; assertive, hard-nosed yes, but not ruthless. I don't want to damage our company's reputation by coming off like vultures," Kingston explained.

Sanaa paused before responding, glancing again at the website and paying particular attention to those who made up the leadership of the company. Kingston's concern was telling in a way uncommon to most CEO's of multimillion-dollar companies.

"If there is going to be fallout, that can be managed," Sanaa suggested. "But instead of focusing on how the business world would perceive the takeover, consider the employees who are potentially in flux; unsure if they will have a job because the leadership can't get their shit together." Sanaa heard Kingston chuckle. "Oh, apologies for the language," she began. "The environment made me more comfortable than the board room."

"No apologies necessary," Kingston smiled. "The truth is the truth," he stated. "And as far as the shift in focus is concerned, that's a great way to look at things; takes the negative spin off the takeover."

"How much will the acquisition cost the company, if you don't mind me asking," Sanaa queried.

"I welcome your inquiries," Kingston answered. "I think we can acquire the company for eighteen to twenty million."

That's sexy as hell, Sanaa thought. A man that had the heart to be concerned about others, and the wealth and knowledge to wield the kind of finance Kingston did? That was sexy as hell. Kingston was a powerful man, but his was a quiet power that was even more alluring to Sanaa. Kingston, although a reputable CEO, was not the kind of man one would see at the hot spots in the city, or on the covers of tabloid magazines with a variety of women on his arm. Kingston could if that was his nature. He was handsome enough. He was fine enough. The kinds of covers Kingston did grace were those that touted his business accouterment, his generous philanthropic endeavors, and entrepreneurial savvy. Quiet, humble, confident and incredibly sexy. For Sanaa, she would have instantly recognized the sexy. The other characteristics although present would have never mattered because Sanaa hadn't been interested in venturing much deeper than the façade of a man. That's all men were anyway; facades and fronts. Short term encounters didn't require seeing past that to anything else. At least it hadn't been. That Sanaa noticed the nuances of Kingston was a cognitive shift for her. It was a first. Those were Sanaa's ruminations as the conversation continued.

"And the projected return in the first three years, assuming it will take that long for your company to see a return," Sanaa continued.

"I would certainly hope the financial return would occur prior to that timeframe," Kingston replied. "However, the primary goal is to stabilize the company and the workforce, bolstering their confidence within the first six to eight months. The second level return that we hope will materialize will be the gateway to the Canadian market and beyond. And lastly, acquisition of green space acreage in that peninsula."

"With that being said, then, what is it that you need from Pinnacle?" Sanaa inquired.

Kingston sat back in his chair. He always had an appreciation for intellectual stimulation; something he'd found missing from too many female encounters in the past. Or, the woman would have some semblance of who he was and present with a Google search version of interest. But there was no real, authentic exchange; no real depth to the conversation. With Sanaa, though, she was smart, and there was a depth to her intelligence that Kingston found irresistible.

I don't need anything from Pinnacle, really," Kingston blatantly admitted. "But, Pinnacle has you." There was so much conviction and possessiveness in Kingston's voice that Sanaa's heart thumped in response. Instinctively, Sanaa averted Kingston's gaze which was an uncommon response for her since she considered herself emotionally impenetrable. Sanaa's eyes did find Kingston's, though. When she did, her heart thumped recklessly again. Kingston's appraisal was sure; seeing past Sanaa's self-imposed defenses and into the core of her soul. Sanaa felt unsettled by the intensity of Kingston's gaze but countered her feelings with an instinctual pouty smile. Kingston saw the smile reaching Sanaa's eyes, and there was a melt to his heart as he recognized the vulnerability underneath.

"Pinnacle has me because they were clear about wanting me," Sanaa cooed.

Kingston's thick brow lifted, and his lips curved sexily.

"Then, let me be clear," Kingston strummed. "I want you."

"When did you come to this Kingston?" Sanaa challenged. She remembered the previous rejections, feeling an edge of hurt from the sting of that.

He reached for her hand. Kingston wanted Sanaa to feel what he was about to say as much as she heard what he had to say. There was a slight reluctance in Sanaa accepting Kingston's hand. But he was willing to wait for Sanaa; to let Sanaa know that he was there for her whether she believed him or not. A part of Sanaa wanted her resistance to be obvious. At no point did she want Kingston to have the impression that she was easy, especially if she was not in control. The control eliminated easiness because Sanaa directed the situation. Kingston denied her of control. Sanaa found it hard to relinquish. She hadn't considered giving up anything, just taking what she wanted and discarding the rest. The rest of who the masculine presence was never mattered before. Truthfully, Sanaa didn't want it to matter now. Was there mixed messaging? Possibly, but that was a result of Sanaa's emotional reluctance. She struggled to admit emotionality even existed. Sanaa did eventually take Kingston's upturned hand. He held her hand, covering Sanaa's completely in his own. The touch was intensely provocative and magical. They both felt the current running between them.

"There has never been a question in my mind that I wanted you, beautiful. I've known that since the beginning," Kingston answered. "You didn't give my desire a chance," Kingston continued; the seductiveness of his baritone voice washing over Sanaa. "You had an agenda."

The forthrightness of his response was bold. Sanaa wasn't used to being the recipient of such directness as most of the men she'd dealt with in the past said what they thought she wanted to hear because they had the same goal as Sanaa did. They wanted the physical and would do and say whatever was necessary to gain the ultimate contact with her; ultimate for them, calculated for Sanaa. Yet, Kingston's honesty was intriguingly refreshing. He stood up to Sanaa. Could she be as honest?

"We've strayed away from business," Sanaa replied. Her answer wasn't as defensive as the words suggested.

"Stay here with me, beloved," Kingston encouraged, caressing Sanaa's hand in his own.

I can't, was Sanaa's prevailing thought. She wanted to pull her hand away and resist the place Kingston was trying to take her.

"What if I don't want to," Sanaa whispered. To stay as Kingston suggested was a struggle. Honestly, Sanaa felt like she was pushed onto her back, showing her underbelly, surrendering to an unrelenting attacker.

"I have to respect it if that's your decision," Kingston acknowledged. "Just know I won't let it go. If I have to drag you kicking and screaming, Sanaa, I will get in. I will get to know the real you." Kingston's brooding eyes continued to bore through her.

Sanaa fought against her natural predilection for questioning what Kingston said; to beleaguer the point with why, and to challenge his masculine authority. Appreciating his alpha tendencies was reserved to the physical, the swagger and attractiveness of his presentation. She didn't want to address the alpha of his emotions, his compelling manner which pushed Sanaa to vulnerability, relinquishing her own authority in the matter. But, Kingston's push was not forceful or violent or inconsiderate. He was demanding in another way; unexpectedly compassionate, yet, heartfully insistent.

"I don't know what to say," Sanaa quietly admitted.

Her level of reserve was heartwarming for Kingston.

"Don't say anything," Kingston replied. "Come, let's take a walk."

Sanaa's eyes widened, and there was a pitch to a single arched brow.

"It's cold," Sanaa announced.

"I won't let you freeze," Kingston answered. "Come with me."

"You better not," Sanaa threatened with her eyes lifting to trace Kingston's frame as he stood from his chair. Kingston eased Sanaa's chair back and waited until she was standing and had stepped aside before replacing the chair under the table. Kingston reached for Sanaa's hand, and she looked back briefly over her shoulder towards the table as Kingston led Sanaa out of the office.

Chapter Ten

*a*s the duo crossed the main hall and into the next room, Sanaa was immediately taken by the sweeping views from the picture windows that seemed to go on forever; so much so that Zeus' presence in the room didn't even phase her. The roaring fire in the smooth stone fireplace that reached the height of the soaring ceiling brought an additional bit of warmth and coziness Sanaa didn't want to leave.

"If our walk was across to this room, then it was wonderful. Thank you for that," Sanaa quipped with a wink and unintended sexy smile.

"You are funny aren't you," Kingston strummed.

"Sometimes," Sanaa sang as she strolled closer to the warming fire. Kingston laughed as he crossed the room, temporarily leaving Sanaa's sight. Hearing Kingston' returning footfalls against the shiny hardwood floor drew Sanaa's eye.

"What do you have there," Sanaa asked, seeing the bowed boxes in Kingston's large hands.

"I said I wouldn't let you freeze," Kingston replied, sitting the boxes on the side table near Sanaa.

"For me," Sanaa asked, pointing at herself.

"Yes, Sanaa, these are for you," Kingston answered.

Slowly, she padded towards Kingston and her gifts. Sanaa had to quiet her suspicious nature. In the past when a man did something nice for Sanaa, gave her a gift, there was an expectation of return. Typically, Sanaa would ask, with enough umption in her voice for the person to know she thought him untrustworthy. Sanaa avoided that compunction and offered a genuinely pleasant smile instead. Kingston took a step back giving Sanaa room to open her packages. She pulled the silky turquoise bow on the first chocolate brown box and then lifted the lid.

Sanaa lifted the tissue paper and then took a step back, her eyes slowly trailing to his. Kingston saw the surprise in her eyes that seemed to erase the distrust.

"Kingston," Sanaa sighed, gingerly stepping back toward the package. She peered in again and then couldn't take her eyes off Kingston. She searched the depths of his eyes for his reason. There was a moment where the two were perfectly quiet. Kingston was settled and willing to let the silence of his voice and the fullness of his gaze to answer whatever questions Sanaa may have had. Sanaa wasn't as comfortable with the silence; not because she couldn't handle the quiet but because of the internal noise in her head and her heart that made her uncomfortable.

"Let me help you," Kingston suggested as he saw Sanaa's eyes soften. Sanaa placed a hand to her belly as if to settle it. Kingston lifted the three-quarter faux fur sable from the box. The coat was even more stunning in full view. Sanaa still couldn't wrap her mind around Kingston. She stood still as he walked behind her and gently placed the luxurious coat on her shoulders, encouraging her to extend her arms and accept the silk-lined gift. The coat fit Sanaa like a glove.

"How did you know my size? How did you know I would come?"

"Do you like it?" Kingston crooned, lightly tracing the fur on her shoulders with his fingertips.

"This coat is amazing," Sanaa cooed, "but that doesn't answer my question."

"Chauncey is wonderful, and she helped," Kingston admitted smilingly.

"She is so fired when I get back," Sanaa quipped.

Kingston grabbed Sanaa by the shoulders and gently spun her around, so she faced him.

"You will do no such thing," Kingston insisted.

"Chauncey is culpable in setting me up," Sanaa snided trying hard not to smile.

"True, but she had a good reason," Kingston answered, "and I can be quite persuasive."

"What did you bribe her with?"

"Kingston laughed heartily. "I didn't bribe Chauncey," Kingston answered. "Maybe she sees what I see, that there is something special between us. Maybe Chauncey is a hopeless romantic."

"Like you," Sanaa sassed.

"Something to that effect," Kingston replied.

"Then why would she tell you things about me, like my size? Which is intimately personal by the way," Sanaa quipped.

"You are a beautiful size, Sanaa," Kingston replied gazing down into her eyes.

"Let me call her and see what you bribed her with," Sanaa slithered, taking a step out of Kingston's radius.

"Sanaa, stop," Kingston suggested.

"Where's my phone?" She insisted, trying to retrace her steps mentally.

"Sanaa," Kingston said with an extra layer of bass in his voice. Sanaa spun abruptly on her heels, and a manicured hand landed on her hip. She felt the suppleness of the exquisite coat under her fingers. When she rolled her eyes,

Kingston laughed; the heartiness of his voice filling the expanse of the room.

"Leave Chauncey alone and open the rest of your gifts. We are supposed to be going for a walk."

"And what if I didn't come? What if I didn't show up? What would you have done with these gifts then?"

"I would have found another opportunity to give them to you. I bought them for you. I would make sure you got them."

"You don't' tell me what to do," Sanaa asserted.

Kingston stroked his chin slowly and methodically as he took a few determined but calculated steps forward.

"You say that beautiful," Kington answered, stepping forward again eradicating the distance between them. "Yet, you like it when I do."

She sized him up, her eyes shifting from one of his to the other trying to catch Kingston flinching. But no matter how deeply Sanaa probed, Kingston was firm; his eyes were firm and piercing.

"You don't have to admit it, beautiful, but I would like you to open the rest of your gifts."

The witty comeback was on the tip of her tongue. She had to have one because that's who Sanaa was. She never let a man get away with bossing her around. Sanaa was used to being the one in charge. Still, there was a part of Sanaa that liked Kingston's authoritative stance. Again, she found him sexy in an unexpected and unyielding way. Acquiescing is not what Sanaa did, ever. This time, though, Sanaa was willing to. She said as much.

"This time," Sanaa groaned after squaring off with Kingston. "But don't get used to it."

"I want you to get used to it," Kingston rebuffed without a second thought. "I want you to get used to the idea of accepting that I am a man; a man who knows what I want. I am a man, beautiful, and I am used to pursuing who and what I want. I pursue, Sanaa, and in my pursuit of what I want, who I want, I must be in control. I must be insistent. I have to be the Alpha man; the alpha you seek but refuse to admit is what you like," Kingston persisted. "I want your willingness in my pursuit of you."

"And if I'm not willing?" Sanaa challenged.

"You are," Kingston whispered, as he reeled Sanaa into him; pushing past her passive resistance and wrapping his muscled arms around the taut of Sanaa's waist. He lowered his mouth to hers and stopped just a whisper away from kissing Sanaa's inviting lips.

"You are."

When he leaned in and claimed the lips he craved, Kingston did so with such intensity it took Sanaa's breath away. She felt the strength of his chest as he breathed heavily against her, probing her mouth with his tongue and tasting her sweet essence. Kingston felt the rise of Sanaa's lovely bosom against his chest as he devoured her lips and sucked on her tongue. Kingston needed to make it clear that he was sincere and earnest in his pursuit. Feeling Sanaa relax into him; drop the rigidity of her resistance emboldened Kingston and his kiss became feverish. The quickening of her breathing pulsed through him and his dick responded to her nearness. Sanaa felt his manhood pressing against her and the tingle in her jewel.

After the heated fervor and the intimacy of their kiss, Kingston ended their entanglement with a soft, feathery kiss to Sanaa's lips.

"Now, open your gifts."

Sanaa rolled her eyes, but there was a smile still on her lips. "You make me sick," Sanaa snided, "for real."

Kingston smiled as Sanaa turned to the remaining packages and opened them. There was a faux fur hat to match her new coat and a muff to cover her hands. There was also a pair of snow boots to replace the leather boots Sanaa wore. Kingston kneeled after encouraging Sanaa to sit and removed her boots replacing them with the ones he purchased. He was gentle with Sanaa; careful with her.

"Are you ready for our walk now," Kingston asked extending a hand to help Sanaa from the seat. Her eyes trailed to the window. The sun seemed lower than it was when she entered the estate.

"It looks so cold out there," Sanaa observed.

"You'll be plenty warm, I promise," Kingston reassured.

"And if I'm not," Sanaa questioned as they strolled to the main hallway and towards the back of the mansion.

"If you aren't, I will do whatever is necessary to fix it," Kington promised as he opened the French doors for the duo to exit.

"You better," Sanaa smiled.

As soon as the door to the outside was opened, Sanaa immediately felt the coolness of the breeze stirring. However, Sanaa didn't focus on the worst part of being outside in the cold. That was nearly impossible when she allowed herself to see what lay before her. Kingston kept his eyes on Sanaa as she started to drink it in; the reason Kingston loved the mountains. The backyard if you will, seemed to go on forever. Even with the mounds of snow, the walkways that meandered through the back property were clear.

"How?" Sanaa asked.

Kingston placed his hand near the center of her back as Zeus took to the yard. He frolicked in the snow, seemingly undeniably happy.

"Heat," Kingston answered. "Underneath all the walkways are radiant heat bands much like the ones used in bathrooms to keep the floors warm."

"Very clever," Sanaa replied genuinely impressed.

The two took to the stone steps that were also clear and ventured out into the yard. Sanaa found herself smiling as she watched Zeus. He seemed to be having so much fun. Her hands were warm in the muff, and the coat did keep the chill from penetrating her bones. Kingston seemed perfectly comfortable standing in the vastness of his space. Sanaa marveled at the ebb and flow of the snow that sat atop the hills and mountains in the distance. The tall trees that skirted the property were dusted with snow on their lush green leaves.

"Not so bad, huh," Kingston asked.

"No, to be honest," Sanaa answered. "Still I prefer fall or spring, but this isn't quite as bad as I thought."

"Good to hear," Kingston surmised.

The duo walked full circle enjoying the quiet, and silently enjoying the company. As they neared the stairs, Sanaa spoke.

"I think you should acquire the company, make it right for the employees, and worry about any fallout later."

"Is that Pinnacle's position," Kingston chided.

"Did you really summons me out here for Pinnacle's position?"

"Yes and no," Kingston admitted.

"You really could separate yourself from Pinnacle, run your own firm," Kingston suggested.

Sanaa stopped and gracefully turned to face Kingston.

"I am on the partner track," Sanaa replied. "Pinnacle is a reputable company, and I have added much-needed diversity where there was none."

"And all of that is commendable, beautiful," Kingston affirmed. "Still instead of being on track for partner, you Sanaa Chase, could be CEO of your own firm. You, Ms. Sanaa Chase, have a reputation as an astute stock trader and innovator in your field. You, Ms. Chase, could represent diversity in a way that threatens the very establishment that needs to be infiltrated in a way I am confident would send chills through the old boys' network. You can do that," Kingston suggested.

Again, Sanaa found herself searching Kingston's eyes for the validity of his response. Was he genuine? Were his comments sincere or was there an angle she hadn't considered? But when she looked there didn't seem to be a cloud of hidden agenda laden in his gaze. Kingston's eyes were clear, and his words seemed clearer; speaking to his true nature and not some charade. Sanaa wasn't used to that. No man ever articulated such confidence in Sanaa, in her skill set. No man had ever encouraged her to be more than she was on an intellectual level, not just a physical one. Sanaa wasn't used to that, any of it. She wasn't used to a man like Kingston.

"I will take what you said under advisement," Sanaa replied as they mounted the stairs. "However, in order to strike out on my own, I need a client base."

"You have that, beautiful," Kinston reassured with a kind and brilliant smile. "You have done a formidable job with your clientele, and they would gladly follow you to your own firm," Kingston ensured.

"And you know that how?"

"I did my due diligence before accepting your meeting. I saw what you did with other investors. I know how you handled my company. That was you, Ms. Chase, being your awesome self, putting your clients' needs first, taking on their interests as though they were your own. You didn't do that with my company because of anything other than the way you handle business. You did that for me, and I know you did that for the others. You, Sanaa Chase, have Wells Woods International, and you have me."

Kingston and Sanaa entered the residence. Zeus wasn't quite finished playing yet. Kingston wasn't concerned. Zeus had free reign of the property, but he always returned home. He helped Sanaa out of her coat and her boots and then took off his own.

"Are you hungry," Kingston asked as they made their way to the living room.

"If our business is finished, I should really be heading back" Sanaa suggested.

"That's one way of looking at it," Kingston answered, not faltering in his confident stride.

"Is there another way," Sanaa asked, interested to see what his comeback would be.

"Of course," Kington answered. "We can continue to talk business, intermingle some personal and get to know each other better."

"That way, the business wouldn't necessarily be over. Is that right, Kingston?"

"That's exactly right, Sanaa. With you and me the business would never have to be over. We both thrive on business conquests. Business to us is as natural as breathing and the conversation I hope we will continue would move to and from business to personal to politics to sports to whatever we want to talk about. Just don't leave."

"You think I'm so easily persuaded?"

"I would hope persuasion wasn't necessary at this point, Sanaa."

"I could see how you could make that cognitive leap," Sanaa reasoned.

"Did I presume erroneously? Is there someone you need to get back to?" Kingston knew his question could lead to an answer he didn't want to hear. But he had to trust his gut instinct and that there was sufficient interest on her part that a someone else wouldn't be an issue. Kingston hoped he was right. He would be crushed if he wasn't.

Sanaa took a step forward then continued to pace making a circle around Kingston. This was the first time since they'd been together that Kingston didn't sound quite as confident in his stance. There was a hint of a question in his voice. The old Sanaa would have capitalized on the opportunity; on what she perceived to be a weakness. But she didn't have that shrewd desire in her heart to dominate and annihilate.

"Is there someone I need to get back to," Sanaa repeated. "There are a few people who might become concerned if I didn't return," Sanaa smiled, steepling her fingers as she continued to pace around him. "Chauncey being one of them."

"And the other," he precariously wagered.

She waited to respond. Kingston wasn't weak; he was interested. Sanaa could see that.

"My best friend," Sanaa finally replied.

Kingston exhaled. He tried to be cognizant of how loudly, but he did exhale relieved that he'd been right that Sanaa wasn't otherwise involved.

"Then there's no reason for you not to stay. Call Chauncey and your best friend. Let them know you're okay. And then, decide that you'll stay here with me," Kingston suggested.

Sanaa stopped pacing, landing directly in front of Kingston. Looking up into his dark eyes, Sanaa smiled with her eyes first and then the slightest turn of her full lips.

"I can do that."

Chapter Eleven

"Hey, you," Tempestt sang as she answered the phone.

"Hey girl," Sanaa replied. She'd taken her cell phone into the luxurious first-floor restroom.

"What's up with you," Tempestt asked. "After our last conversation, I wasn't sure how soon I would hear from you."

"I'm used to you preaching and lecturing me," Sanaa sighed. "I can't hold that against you for too long."

"Good to know," Tempestt laughed. "So, what's up? Still at the office?"

Sanaa smiled. "Not quite," she answered.

Tempestt heard something in Sanaa's voice.

"Exactly what does that mean," Tempestt asked, ensuring the phone was snug to her ear, so she didn't miss anything.

Sanaa padded in long circles around the spacious restroom; taking note of the shiny knobs and pleasing decorum. The scent of jasmine hung fragrantly in the air.

"He summoned me," Sanaa admitted.

"Who? The lumber king?"

"Girl yes, the lumber king," Sanaa sighed exaggeratedly.

"Where are you, Sanaa?"

"You wouldn't believe me if I told you," Sanaa laughed.

"Oh, I have to know now," Tempestt giggled.

"I am in Colorado, girl. In the boonies."

Tempestt didn't respond with words. At first, her mouth fell open. Sanaa and the cold? Not a good mix. Then she started to laugh, covering her mouth so Sanaa couldn't fully hear her.

"I hear you," Sanaa frowned.

"I'm sorry, girl," Tempestt giggled. "Tell me it's cold and snowy?"

"All you see is white," Sanaa explained. "As far as the eye can see it's all white, T. And cold? Oh my god. It's a different kind of cold than what we're used to. This some for real cold. And you ain't shit for laughing, either," Sanaa scoffed.

That made Tempestt laugh even harder. As they say, laughter is infectious, and Sanaa found herself laughing, too.

"Whatever Tempestt" Sanaa chided. "He got me out here in the damn wilderness. But I thought I should at least let someone know where I was, just in case."

"Don't even try to sound pressed by that," Tempestt clapped back.

"Like I said, whatever. It's business."

"Mmhmm," Tempestt mumbled. "Business or whatever it is, you are there for a reason. Try to have a good time," Tempestt replied, not paying attention to the feigned disdain in Sanaa's voice.

"Mmhmm," Sanaa groaned. "I'll talk to you later."

"Have fun!" Tempestt encouraged before hanging up the phone. She smiled even after the line disconnected. More than anything, Tempestt wanted for Sanaa what she wanted for herself. Tempestt wanted Sanaa to be twice as happy as she was. Sanaa deserved it, and Tempestt prayed that she would have it.

Before leaving the restroom, Sanaa shot a quick text to Chauncey.

When Sanaa's phone buzzed in her hand, and she looked at Chauncey's response; a line of smiling emoji's, Sanaa rolled her eyes and then burst out laughing. Sanaa would chastise Chauncey later, but she smiled, nonetheless. After washing her hands, Sanaa returned to the family room. There was an aroma in the air that enticed her senses. As she padded around the couch, Kingston was stretched out in front of the fireplace with a veritable smorgasbord spread out on a picnic style blanket.

"I hope you don't mind the informality," Kingston said as he extended his hand for Sanaa to sit down on the blanket next to him. "But I thought a picnic style dinner to give you feelings of summer by the warm fire would help block out the cold."

"Thoughtful," Sanaa replied, getting comfortable on the blanket. "I'm glad I have elastic in the waist of my pants. The food looks and smells delicious," Sanaa smiled as her eyes trailed across the spread.

"We have lobster rolls, passion fruit curd on Breusch, goat cheese with fig and pear, caviar, fresh strawberries, champagne and my one indulgence, Sweet Surrender D'Or cupcakes flown in from Las Vegas," Kingston explained.

"Those cupcakes look like expensive jewels," Sanaa replied. The Sweet Surrender cupcakes boasted a brushed gold cap trimmed in tiny edible pearls suspended above the cake covered in chocolate ganache housed in a midnight blue cup trimmed with edible gold leaf.

"Wait until you taste them," Kingston replied.

"I can't wait."

"Shall I say grace," Kingston suggested.

"Of course, Sanaa willingly agreed.

She accepted Kingston's extended hand and felt the warmth of his fingertips as they interlaced with hers.

"Faithful God, thank you for your blessings and protections, seen and unseen. Thank you for the bounty of the food before us. Thank you for the hands that prepared it. Let it be nourishing for our bodies and food to our souls, amen."

"Amen," Sanaa agreed.

The food was just as delicious as it looked. Kingston enjoyed watching Sanaa eat, and he loved it when she got really quiet and focused when something was good to her. Sanaa didn't quite hum when she was eating happily, but she did rock from side to side, just a little. You had to pay close attention to notice, and Kingston did.

"I don't think I can eat another bite," Sanaa sighed, sitting back and resting her palms on the comfortable blanket.

"What about dessert," Kingston asked wiping the corners of his mouth with the linen napkin.

"Can we save it for later?"

"Sure, beautiful," Kingston answered.

"Since you served, let me help you clear things up," Sanaa offered.

"Thanks for that," Kingston said standing to his full height and then extending his hand as Sanaa stood up. They gathered the dishes and the dessert and made their way to the gourmet kitchen near the back of the estate.

"How often are you in Colorado," Sanaa asked, leaning against the counter.

"Every chance I get," Kingston replied.

The kitchen was state of the art. There didn't seem to be one thing out of place. It was pristine as though rarely used. Their conversation continued as Kingston led Sanaa to another part of the house. They entered the den, brimming with books in mahogany bookcases, supple leather chairs and a comfortable chaise style couch position directly across from another spectacular fire. On the side table was a snifter of brandy with two small glasses. Kingston welcomed Sanaa to sit with him on the couch. Once they were comfortable, Kingston filled their glasses, offering one to Sanaa.

"Thank you."

The den also offered amazing views that Sanaa appreciated as she gazed out of the large windows, taking the first sip of brandy.

"Tell me something about you that most people don't know," Kingston asked, draping his muscular arm around the back of the couch.

"Only if you do the same, and go first," Sanaa replied.

"Ah, a quick turn of the tables, huh?"

"Would you expect anything less?" Sanaa offered with a wink.

"No, I wouldn't," Kingston acquiesced. Kingston took a sip of brandy before continuing. "Hmm, something about me that most people don't know."

"Oh, so you ask me a question you're not prepared to answer?" Sanaa asked.

"Anything you want to know about me, just ask," Kingston replied. "Are you willing to say the same?"

"Honestly? I'm not sure," Sanaa replied. "But no deflection. Tell me something."

Kingston nodded but then fell quiet. There was no more witty banter just his quiet contemplation. Sanaa didn't rush him. She could tell this was more than just a general question. Kingston tossed out there to generate conversation.

"I don't want to die alone."

Sanaa's brow furrowed. What Kingston said was nothing Sanaa expected. She turned fully to face him.

"Where did that come from," Sanaa asked.

"I'm not sure," Kington answered. "I feel like I can tell you anything without fluff or filibuster. Maybe because you are so direct and forthright, I can be that with you."

Sanaa nodded. She got that. "Why do you feel that way? You're young, vibrant, handsome; what makes you think that would even happen?"

"Genuine connection," Kingston replied. "The woman I desire a genuine connection with fights me on every turn. I can see a future with her, but I don't know. She's tough," Kingston continued. "If I don't win her over soon, I won't have a lifetime to spend with her."

"Maybe there's a reason she's tough," Sanaa uttered.

"Maybe she's willing to talk about it," Kingston encouraged.

Pausing, Sanaa took another sip of brandy. She felt an uncomfortable churn in her gut.

"Maybe she's concerned his feelings would change."

"Maybe she should trust that they won't."

"Maybe it's too embarrassing," Sanaa whispered. Her gut churned again. She felt vulnerable even though she hadn't revealed a thing.

"He wouldn't dare judge," Kingston answered, placing a gentle hand on her shoulder.

Why do I even want to tell you, to open up to you," Sanaa whined, folding in half and resting her head on her knees. "I don't even know you like that."

Kingston's comforting hand followed her and rested on the center of Sanaa's back.

"Sometimes there's a heart connection, a soul connection even before we recognize it," Kingston offered.

Slowly, Sanaa sat up. "And you believe that?"

Kingston extended his finger, placing it under Sanaa's chin and inclining her face to him.

"I do."

Sanaa breathed in deeply, exhaling slowly. "I need another drink if I'm going to spill my guts," she sighed, lifting her glass for a refill. Kingston obliged. Sanaa drank from the glass and then rested it between both hands.

"She's tough because she had no choice. She's tough because that's how she survived; how she continues to survive. She doesn't trust easily because her trust was broken early. She has to protect herself because the one person she thought she could count on to do that, chose him instead."

Kingston felt the weightiness of Sanaa's words and heard the bridled pain in her voice. There was an ache in his heart for what Sanaa said and what she omitted. Sanaa felt the press of hot tears against the back of her eyes. Unwilling to shed them, Sanaa lifted her glass and emptied it, feeling the burn of the amber liquid going down her throat and into her unsettled belly. Sanaa was emptying herself of the things she'd never shared with any man before. Interestingly, speaking about herself in the third person helped to mentally distance herself; yet, Sanaa still felt the stinging pain. Sanaa wasn't sure how to feel about that, even as she continued.

"Control is better than vulnerability. Youth made her vulnerable. She refused to be that again as an adult. She refused to be hurt anymore."

Hearing Sanaa say those things aloud made so much sense to Kingston. There was silence once again between them. Yet, Kingston's hand near the small of Sanaa's back was somehow reassuring. He didn't pull away from her. She didn't notice alarm on his face or a change in his bodily position. Instead of expected rejection, Kingston leaned in to gain Sanaa's eyes. When he did, he asked permission without saying a word to pull her into him; to allow Sanaa the chance to rest on his strength. Kingston consoled Sanaa for pains he didn't fully comprehend. That didn't matter to him though. He didn't have to have the full scope of who hurt her. What Kingston knew is that Sanaa was hurting. Her hurt pained him. Sanaa lifted her legs onto the sofa, and she laced her arm around Kingston's waist. He wrapped the strength of his arm around her and cradled Sanaa.

She really expected some form of judgment, maybe even nonverbal rejection; the subtle kind; an errant look, a disapproving stare when she wasn't looking. Kingston hadn't responded that way. The suspicious side of Sanaa that she couldn't fully suppress lingered.

"Thank you, beautiful," Kingston whispered kissing Sanaa lightly on the forehead.

"For what," Sanaa asked.

"For your willingness, for your openness," Kingston replied. "I know that wasn't easy for you." Kingston stroked Sanaa's curly locs as he spoke.

"I still don't know why I told you," Sanaa sighed.

"But you did, which says something," Kingston crooned.

"That identifying soul's thing, huh?"

"I would like to think so," Kingston answered.

Sanaa yawned unexpectedly. "Oh, excuse me," she apologized.

"No need," Kingston answered. "It's been a long day. Come, beautiful. Let me show you to the guest room."

Sanaa uncurled from Kingston, and he helped her stand up.

"Can I take my cupcake with me?"

Kingston smiled. "Of course, you can."

Kingston escorted Sanaa up the floating stairs to the guest suite. The room was just as marvelous as the remainder of the estate. Sanaa's bags were already there.

"There are fresh towels and a robe in the ensuite. If there's anything else you need, I'm right down the hall," Kingston explained. "And thanks again for staying. I love having you here, Sanaa."

"Thanks for your hospitality," Sanaa smiled. "But," Sanaa replied coyly, "would I be too predictable if I said I really don't want you to leave me."

Kingston's brow pitched slightly as he moved closer to Sanaa. "I didn't want to be predictable by saying I don't want to leave you either."

"So, what do we do," Sanaa asked earnestly. This was virgin territory for her.

"Well beautiful, we do whatever we feel is right," Kingston answered.

That's part of the problem, Sanaa thought to herself. Her definition of right and wrong was clouded by years of manipulation.

"You might need to help me with that," Sanaa admitted. She couldn't believe she said it out loud, collapsing on the bed and covering her face. "Was there some truth serum in that brandy? Geesh," Sanaa bemoaned.

"I don't think so," Kingston chortled.

"Ugggh," Sanaa groan again. "I feel like I'm in a Catholic confessional."

"I'm not Catholic," Kingston replied.

"That brandy might be," Sanaa quipped.

They both laughed.

"I have an idea," Kingston began.

"And what is that?"

"A relaxing bubble bath, comfortable pajamas, and warm sheets," Kingston replied.

Sanaa uncovered her face fully and sat up on the bed. "Now that sounds like a good idea," Sanaa agreed as she stood up from the softness of the bed.

Sanaa followed Kingston into the bathroom and was not disappointed in the least with the deep soaking tub and the warmed tiger wood floors. Kingston strolled to the tub and turned on the water.

"I need bubbles," Sanaa grinned.

"Bubbles it is," Kingston answered. "Your choice of scents madam," Kingston offered, showing Sanaa a variety of bottles near the tub. Sanaa accepted his invitation and padded over. There were great choices available to her, but this was a bath they would be sharing. Sanaa didn't want to pick anything too florally, or too girly. Pleased with her selection, Sanaa spun on her heels, turning to the tub and pouring in the fragrance.

"I thought you were going to let me see," Kingston said, playfully reaching for the bottle that Sanaa quickly tucked behind her back. Kingston didn't halt his pursuit, wrapping his arms around Sanaa's waist while trying to lay claim to the bottle.

"Let your nose do the work, Mr. Wells," Sanaa cracked up when Kingston nuzzled against her neck, tickling her into fits of laughter.

"Mmmm," he hummed against the softness of her flesh sending heated pulsations to her core which served to alter the tone of her laughter.

"We should probably check the water level," Sanaa giggled.

"We better," Kingston agreed. Kingston reached over and turned off the water then checked it with his massive hand to check the temperature.

"It's good," Kingston replied, pulling his sudsy hand from the water.

Sanaa reached over to the counter and picked up a towel and then reached over gently wiping the suds from Kington's hand. It was a kind gesture that he appreciated. His eyes said the same as Kingston gazed down and watched Sanaa. She must have felt the penetration of his gaze as she slowly raised her mink-lashed eyes to meet his. Sanaa flushed under the warmth of Kingston's eyes. She replaced the towel on the counter and then turned her smoldering eyes back to Kingston. This time, Sanaa stood face to face with Kingston, returning as intense as gaze as he offered. There was this moment of appreciation between the two of them. They were both being forthright without the utterance of a single word. When Kingston reached up to Sanaa's collar and unbuttoned the first button, Sanaa did the same, reaching to his height and unbuttoning the first button of his shirt.

There was a heightened sexual tension in the room. Kingston smiled as the smell of warmed vanilla filled the room. As he slid Sanaa's blouse from her creamy dark shoulders the smile faded and Kingston folded in his bottom lip, biting down on the flesh before slowly releasing it. Sanaa elevated on tiptoe to ease Kingston's shirt from his broad shoulders. As Sanaa lowered herself taking Kingston's shirt down as she went, her eyes took in the thick of Kingston's shoulders, espousing defined muscles. The rise of Kingston's pecs tapering down to the rippled muscles of his abdomen was enough to cause Sanaa to cross her legs, tightening her thighs feeling her body respond to his overwhelming sexiness.

"I won't be able to get your pants off like that," Kingston whispered as he leaned in and kissed Sanaa's shoulder. Sanaa instinctively squeezed her thighs even tighter; allowing herself to feel his kiss without counterattack. The first moisture from her pulsing jewel sated her lace panties.

"I may have a hard time with yours as well," Sanaa purred, dropping her eyes to the protrusion in Kington's pants. Kingston's eyes didn't need to follow Sanaa's. He felt the thump in his dick and the press for freedom.

"If you'll take your time with me, I'll take my time with you," Kingston crooned.

"Agreed," Sanaa whispered.

Slowly Sanaa unbound her legs as she reached for Kingston's belt. Sanaa traced her finger around Kingston's buckle. Her action drove him nuts. The sexual tension in the room escalated to a new high and Kingston wasn't sure he could keep himself from ravaging the beautiful Sanaa that stood before him. Sanaa heard the difference in Kingston's breathing. He reached for the strap of her lacy bra and eased it from Sanaa's shoulder and then the second. His eyes narrowed as her firm breasts came into view. There was no hesitation in Kingston's next move.

"Mmm," Sanaa whimpered as Kingston's thumbs traced her taut nipples, sending shockwaves down her spine.

Sanaa focused her wavering energy on unbuckling Kingston's belt. She eased down his zipper and reached her hands into the waist of what covered him, releasing his thickened manhood from confinement. Sanaa's eyes widened as she saw his girth and length and her pussy thumped again. Sanaa's hand followed her eyes as she reached out and traced the length of him with soft fingers.

"Sssss," Kingston moaned under her feathery touch. His resistance was shattered, and his resolve completely dissipated. Kingston stepped towards Sanaa and with one motion lifted her by the waist onto his core. Sanaa had no resistance, wrapping her legs around his refined waist and lacing her arms around his neck. When Kingston bypassed the tub, Sanaa dropped her head between her shoulders, allowing herself to be carried away by Kingston. He didn't let the opportunity to devour Sanaa's flesh go to waste. He buried his head into the hollow of Sanaa's elegant neck kissing licking and sucking her wanton flesh. The purr Sanaa uttered sent shudders to Kington's core, and she felt the press of his thick cock underneath her.

Kingston shifted his weight, laying Sanaa down on the bed. Starting with her forehead, Kingston kissed her warmly; making a trail down her nose to Sanaa's full lips, down the length of her neck to her breasts. Taking one in each hand, Kingston rotated his thumb against her hardened nipple with one hand and swallowed the other with his warm mouth. She moaned for him and all thoughts of being in control and manipulating Kingston for her own brief sexual satisfaction evaporated. Kingston lifted himself from Sanaa only long enough to fumble with her pants. She helped him reaching down and pushing her pants from her hips. Kingston grabbed one side and then the other until Sanaa's pants were no longer an interruption. Sanaa's legs opened like magic; unable to resist the throb in her puss.

Kingston's hands moved and captured Sanaa's placing them both over her head. He needed Sanaa to know that his desire for her was real. Kingston needed Sanaa to know that being vulnerable with him was not weakness. Kingston needed her to know that she was more to him than a conquest and he wanted to be more than that to her. His eyes conveyed the message, but he wanted Sanaa to understand everything he was thinking clearly.

"I have wanted you, desired you since the beginning." Kingston followed his statement with a lingering kiss to Sanaa's lips as he positioned himself between her thighs; his throbbing manhood just a push away from her welcoming womb.

"I'm not a conquest, and neither are you, Sanaa," Kingston said leveling his gaze to ensure she saw his intent and heard it even more.

"Giving of yourself to me is not one-sided. I'm giving myself to you."

Sanaa was panting; not just from the mind-boggling sexual tension but from the rise of unfiltered emotion that flooded her system. Sanaa was so overwhelmed she couldn't form words. All she could manage was a nod of her head as a single tear trickled down her flushed cheek. Their fingers interlaced as Kingston's lips lowered to touch hers.

Sanaa's folds opened for him. His mouth fell from her mouth to the swell of her breasts. Kingston didn't want to rush. He wanted Sanaa to know he appreciated every part of her; the fullness of Sanaa's womanhood. As Kingston sucked her breast, pulling and nibbling, driving Sanaa to the brink, she gasped as he entered her. Kingston filled her welcoming womb completely. For Kingston, it felt like home, and he branded Sanaa's pussy every chance he got. Everything about Sanaa turned him on, and Kingston couldn't get enough of her. It didn't take long for the two to fall into a natural rhythm. He thrust, she received and pushed back. Cupping her hands behind Kingston's head, Sanaa moved him from her breasts to her mouth. Their lips connected, and their tongues moved in and out, exploring each other's mouths. When Sanaa bit down on Kingston's bottom lip, a surge throttled straight to his loin, and he groaned. Sanaa whispered his name against Kingston's' lips, and another tremble moved through him.

Separating his mouth from hers, Kingston lifted on his knees, placing one of Sanaa's legs on each shoulder. He thrust deeper, hitting her pearl with every masterful stroke. Sanaa whimpered under the thundering pressure and her clitoris pulsed sending the first wave of hot wetness over his shaft.

"Ahh beautiful," Kingston grimaced as his dick swole even more; beads of sweat breaking out on his furrowed brow. Sanaa arched her back and then lifted her hips slightly, giving Kingston unrestricted access to her goodness. He fucked her harder, and Sanaa's hips danced side to side and in circles altering where his push landed. It drove Kingston to the brink. Quivering under his penetration, Sanaa found it hard to catch her breath. Her body was overwhelmed with sensual sensations as Kingston pounded her flesh.

"Kingston, please."

"Please what? What do you want from me, Sanaa," he muttered as the muscles in his thighs tensed and flexed with every stroke. Kingston slowed only long enough to hear her response and look into Sanaa's eyes.

"Take me," Sanaa rasped. "All of me."

A smile eased across Kingston's lips as her words fed his heart and ignited his animalistic instinct. He wanted to drive Sanaa crazy; give all of himself to her in every way possible. Kingston's stroke was focused, intense, and consuming. He pulled his manhood all the way out until just the tip rested in her puss. Fighting the urge to fuck her brains out, Kingston slow pumped Sanaa, making sure she felt every inch of his dick, probing and thumping inside her. He ground his hips and plunged in, to the hilt. Just when Sanaa's body got accustomed to the sensation, Kingston shifted gears again, fast fucking her; Sanaa's ass slapping against his muscled thighs. She squealed as her eyes rolled to the back of her head.

Tension mounted at the base of Kingston's manhood and the veins along his shaft swole.

"GRRRRRR!"

His guttural growl erupted from the pit of his stomach as Kingston unleashed a hot stream of cum into Sanaa's jewel. But he didn't stop fucking her until her climax matched his.

"Kingston!" She screamed, as her body released wave after wave of hot gism. Her panting matched his and beads of sweat from Kingston's brow dropped onto Sanaa's belly. Reaching up, she wiped his forehead as he lowered himself collapsing onto her. Sanaa's legs folded around him and she held him close until their breathing syncopated and slowed. She caressed Kingston's muscular back; feeling the weight of him on her. Sanaa had never been one to cuddle. She never met a man that deserved the time after she got what she wanted. Admittedly, this time for Sanaa was different. And she realized something. Sanaa was as sexually satisfied, even more so than when she had been in control. Sanaa shook her head, and there was a slight curl to her upper lip. Kingston wasn't supposed to be so good. He wasn't supposed to be so capable. Kingston wasn't supposed to give Sanaa all the feels. But, he did.

Chapter Twelve

*N*either Kingston nor Sanaa realized just how tired they were. The two fell asleep in each other's arms. Kingston was the first to stir. Waking up lying between Sanaa's thighs was a welcomed way to open his eyes. Kingston did his best to lift himself from Sanaa with as little disturbance as possible. Sanaa stirred but only turned over and curled up in the fetal position in the absence of Kingston's presence.

As quietly as he could, Kingston padded to the restroom, released the water from the tub, cleaned it, and then refilled the tub putting in more vanilla bubble bath. Kingston made his way back to Sanaa who was still cutely curled up. Kingston couldn't resist lying down next to Sanaa and spooning her as he kissed her ear. She nestled back against Kingston and snuggled in. Kingston felt the press of Sanaa's firm ass against his manhood. But more than that Kingston felt how relaxed Sanaa was, how her guard was down, and how extremely beautiful she really was. To wake her when she was so comfortable would be cruel. Kingston could get used to Sanaa being pressed against him, trusting him, being comforted by him.

Sanaa rustled again. There was a light moan and then a

sigh that was nocturnal music to Kington's ears. When she stretched, Kingston accommodated the shift in her body.

"Is it morning?" Sanaa whispered.

"Not quite beautiful," Kingston crooned. "But I did rerun our bath."

"Mmm, okay," Sanaa hummed. "I'm coming."

"It doesn't sound like it, beautiful," Kingston chortled.

"I know," Sanaa sang. "This bed is so good."

"The bath will be good, too," Kingston assured.

"I'm sure," Sanaa moaned. "It's your fault though."

"How is that," Kingston asked, cradling the fullness of Sanaa's body with his.

"Because you were better than good," Sanaa purred.

"Mmm," Kingston crooned. "And to think, you wanted a quick hit," Kingston smiled.

Sanaa pushed her ass against Kingston and stretched out in his arms. "And now I want seconds."

"Such a bad girl," Kingston moaned.

"And you like it," Sanaa sassed as she turned over in Kingston's arms. Sanaa pressed against him until her weight was shifted on top of Kingston.

"I more than like it," Kingston replied as he adjusted underneath her. His dick was growing thick with the nearness of her mound. Sanaa didn't wait for his hardness to increase. Bending down she lightly kissed Kingston's full lips and brushed her pert nipples against his hard chest. Kingston's hands fell to the roundness of Sanaa's ass as she hungrily devoured his mouth. With the skill and the strength of her thighs, Sanaa positioned Kingston's manhood, shifting her hips until the tip of his dick was inside her folds. Kingston groaned from the touch as Sanaa slowly descended on his fulness. And the swirl of her sexy hips caused his shaft to grow inside her, filling the capacity of Sanaa's folds. But Sanaa wasn't interested in gentility. She wanted a ruckus fuck. Lifting her lips from his and planting her hands solidly on Kingston's chest, Sanaa planted her feet on each side of his frame and found her stroke. The veins of his thickness throbbed as Sanaa tightened her inner walls on the downstroke and flexed her walls on the upstroke. She shifted from fast to slow to fast again as her head fell between her shoulders and Sanaa's titties bounced in the air.

"Shit," Sanaa groaned as Kingston spread her ass cheeks gripping them tightly.

"Grrr," Kingston growled as her ass slapped against his balls. He lifted his hips and moving his hands from Sanaa's ass to her waist, grinding up inside her. She may have been on top, but Kingston took control. Sanaa's head dropped between her shoulders, and she balanced herself placing her hands on his tight thighs.

"Shit, shit, shit," Sanaa panted. "Bae!"

A term of endearment in the heat of passion sent Kingston to a higher plane, and he intended to take Sanaa with him. Sanaa felt him flesh to flesh. Sanaa felt his energy pulse through her. Their rhythm was intense and erratic and frenzied, yet with every stroke, they connected and reconnected and connected again. There was a pricking of Sanaa's heart even in the midst of a mind-blowing fuck.

"Ah, Kingston," Sanaa said breathily.

"Beautiful," Kington groaned.

Sanaa lifted her head and found Kington's eyes as waves of ecstasy washed over them. Reckless abandon didn't break their gaze as Sanaa's walls convulsed releasing a flood of wetness onto Kingston's erectness just as he emptied every ounce of gism into her. But neither of them was willing to give up their connection. Sanaa held Kington within her and milked his manhood. She collapsed onto his chest, wet with sweat. Sanaa didn't care. Her brow was dotted with perspiration as well. Their breathing finally settled as Kingston wrapped his arms around her.

"I think we'll have to run the bath again," Kingston sighed.

"So ridiculous," Sanaa laughed.

THE FRAGRANT YET CALMING SMELL OF VANILLA FILLED Sanaa's nostrils. The bath water was just hot enough to assuage the ache she didn't realize she had between her thighs. Kingston caused the delightfully painful ache. A smile eased across Sanaa's lips as she rested her head on Kingston's chiseled chest. She felt the strength and the subtlety of his arms wrapped casually around her and Sanaa found herself relaxed and unexpectedly satisfied. She was satisfied. Despite all of Sanaa's bravado and closeted insecurities masked as said bravado, Sanaa found herself in a mental space that she couldn't have seen coming. Her eyes closed slowly as she felt Kingston stroke her curled tresses.

"I'm glad you're here," Kingston crooned.

"Surprisingly, me too," Sanaa quipped.

Kingston flipped water on her, and Sanaa laughed playfully. "Seriously? I got your surprise," Kingston chortled. With smooth dexterity, Kingston lowered his hand and simultaneously turned Sanaa to face him. There was a huge smile still on her lips even though her eyes were wide from the turn. Sanaa looked up and saw the simmer in Kingston's eyes. He captured her very essence every time he looked at her with deep probing eyes.

"Come here, girl," Kingston insisted as he compelled her with his eyes and moved her with his hands. Her wide smile slowly dissipated as Sanaa laced her arms around Kingston's neck. Kingston's mouth was quick and devouring as he pulled Sanaa in with a ravaging kiss; searing her lips with his and sucking her tongue because tasting Sanaa was imperative. The intensity of Kingston's kiss made Sanaa pant, and her nipples harden. The ache in her thighs didn't matter anymore as her pussy convulsed from his nearness and the thickness of his girth pressing hard against her. Sanaa couldn't resist a pulsating dick that compelled her. Kingston slid down underneath her, and she lifted a single leg giving him unequaled access to her jewel.

"Ah," Sanaa squealed as Kingston moved into her, slowly, deliberately; just the tip at first which caused her pussy to moisten. Kingston didn't push inside her. He held her there, keeping Sanaa from advancing his dick inside her. She wanted it; she wanted more. Sanaa wanted Kingston fully inside her. Sanaa's eyes lifted and found his. There was a smile dancing at the corner of his lips. Kingston was teasing her, taunting her. She whimpered as her pussy thumped from anticipation and want.

"Uhn," Sanaa moaned.

"Still surprised?" Kingston chaffed.

"You are cruel," Sanaa griped as her pert nipples pressed against Kingston's chest. Her legs tightened, and her body reacted automatically. There was a bounce in Sanaa that she needed to exercise as the tip of Kingston's manhood rested between her pussy lips. Sanaa's eyes were pleading as she lowed her arms and placed her hands against Kingston's chest. Her eyes narrowed, and she folded in her bottom lip. She pushed against Kingston's resistance, demanding that he fill her womb to capacity. Kingston held firm. Holding her in abeyance as her body insisted. They were locked in a desirous stare. Her strength couldn't override his. But Kingston appeased Sanaa by pushing into her an inch more.

"Ahhh!" Sanaa's body quaked when a roaring climax shot through her.

"Still surprised," Kingston asked again, pulling out of Sanaa until she didn't feel him anymore.

"Ahh, ahh!" She moaned as he gave himself back to her, pushing his cock further inside Sanaa, but not more than he had given her before.

Her eyes dropped as her body cried out. There was a tightening in Sanaa's belly and an ache in what felt like her soul. Vulnerability was for weaklings; yet, Sanaa couldn't brace herself against what she felt.

"King, please," she pleaded as her arms could no longer hold her weight and she collapsed into him.

"Please what," Kingston uttered, giving her a little more dick to consider.

"Ewww damn," Sanaa groaned.

But Kingston was unrelenting; denying his own desire to fuck the shit out of her; to satisfy his base primal instinct and devour the puss he craved so much.

"Please what," Kingston insisted with neither his face nor his voice giving away the fact that he wanted desperately to plunge inside Sanaa's depths.

"Fuck me," Sanaa confessed as her eyes returned to find his. Kingston could see the craving in her dark brown pools.

"No." His answer was not what Sanaa expected to hear. It was certainly not what she wanted to hear.

"I don't want to fuck you, beautiful," Kingston explained with his baritone voice sending quivers down her spine as he wrapped his arm fully around her taut waist.

Without taking his eyes from Sanaa until the last second, Kingston adjusted Sanaa's leg, so she was on her side without losing contact with her throbbing jewel. Once again, Kingston moved underneath her, spooning her as the water lapped gently around them, cocooning them in vanilla warmth. Slowly, Kingston gave Sanaa the fullness of his manhood, inch by inch with a determined penetrating grind. Sanaa grabbed the side of the tub as their bodies undulated in perfect sync.

"Then what is this," Sanaa whispered hotly, her mouth falling open from the depths at which Kingston penetrated her; hitting her pearl and staying there with a pronounced stroke.

"You tell me," Kingston whispered into her ear as he lifted her leg gaining access to Sanaa's very soul. His brow was furrowed as Kingston moved inside her walls, feeling them coaxing his cock and heating up every thrust. The grip Sanaa had on the tub tightened as she pushed against his thickness to the hilt. Her body shuddered, and her head fell back.

"What is this, beautiful," Kingston growled against her.

"I don't know," Sanaa cried out; her mind clouded, her thoughts jumbled, her heart racing and her body longing. Sanaa's toes curled as he pushed into her and then pushed against, lifting her with the strength of his stroke.

"What is this," Kingston insisted. "Tell me what you feel, Sanaa."

"I can't," she whimpered and winced from how Kingston made her body feel; how he made her heart feel. Despite how bad Sanaa wanted to deny that her heart was in it, she couldn't. The heart feeling was overwhelming.

"Tell me beautiful," Kingston persisted. "I need you to tell me."

He stroked her again, and again and again; just as slowly, just as deeply, just as measured. That made it even harder for Sanaa to formulate her thoughts let alone her words. She shook her head as if that would help to clear her mind, but it was pointless. It didn't help at all. the fluttering in Sanaa's gut didn't help at all. The pounding of her heart didn't help at all. She never remembered a time her heart beat so hard and so fast to the point that it felt like her heart would burst. Sanaa was breathless.

"King," she gasped. Hearing his name pour from her pouty lips sent a wave of unfiltered desire over Kingston.

"Tell me, beautiful... tell me."

She could hear the angst in his voice. His body was firmly behind her, and she felt a tense and tightening. There was an insistence in his touch and in his voice. Sanaa felt the same urgency as her body gave in to too much goodness all at once. As confusing as it was, Sanaa couldn't hold back anymore.

"...love..."

At that moment, it was as though time stood still. Kingston held her with such conviction that the little breath Sanaa had left was snatched away. She gave in to everything her body held on to. Sanaa gave in to everything her heart couldn't say. She let go of it all in that very moment. He came for her. She came for him. They each felt the heated warmth pour from the other.

Chapter Thirteen

$\mathcal{S}$anaa looked out of the window, thirty thousand feet in the air and saw nothing. It didn't matter though. That's what the persistent smile on her face said. The stewardess had been by a few times. The first time she asked if Ms. Chase wanted anything. It took Sanaa a minute to respond. She didn't hear the stewardess. In Sanaa's mind, she was still laid out in front of Kingston's bedroom fireplace, naked in his arms, enjoying the beat of his heart against the pleasant silence. When she did take note of the stewardess trying to get her attention, Sanaa shook her head. It didn't matter the question. She wanted to stay in the place she had been for the past few days with the man who made her heart do crazy things, and her body respond in even crazier ways.

But all good things must come to an end, right? Both she and Kingston had to return to the reality of their crazy, busy, exciting lives. Sanaa didn't even miss her cell phone when she was with Kingston which was not like her at all. Any other time it would have been like an extension of her appendage, responding to clients checking the market, keeping Chauncey busy. She was in no real rush to turn it on either. Sanaa would, once the plane landed, but for the moment, Sanaa was happy with her head in the clouds reminiscing on the amazement of the past weekend.

Parting was such sweet sorrow, though; at least that's how it felt when the time came for her and Kingston to part ways. Although she felt duped in the beginning, Sanaa realized she would miss being with Kingston. He made it no secret that he would miss her, desperately. This time, when Kingston said, talk soon, after holding her tightly and kissing her passionately, Sanaa wasn't offended, nor did she question his motives. Talk soon didn't ring the second time as it did the first. Sanaa recognized the statement to be a promise; a promise she knew Kingston intended to keep. Sanaa already missed him. She shook her head and smiled as the blue sky passed underneath her. She missed him.

When the plane landed at Hartsfield Jackson, Sanaa was glad for a safe landing. As she walked towards baggage claim, Sanaa turned on her phone. It dinged and pinged with multiple notifications, email, texts and missed calls. She was not surprised to see a call from her boss. With a deep sigh, Sanaa stopped her forward trek and hit redial.

"Mr. Lawrence," Sanaa said as her boss picked up the phone.

"Good to hear from you Ms. Chase," Mr. Lawrence answered. Sanaa ignored the sarcastic undertones in his voice as he continued. "You fell off the radar," Mr. Lawrence added. "Despite that, I hope it works out for Pinnacle."

"The Wells portfolio increased, and Pinnacle is better off for it," Sanaa replied. She could hear the smile on her boss' lips.

"Well done, as always," Mr. Lawrence replied. "I'll see you tomorrow morning."

Sanaa disconnected the line and sashayed down the terminal. Pinnacle would wait until tomorrow. Scrolling through her messages, Sanaa was not surprised that Chauncey left several or that Tempestt called. It would take a minute for the bags to arrive at baggage claim, so Sanaa decided to see what was so pressing from Chauncey. There was one voice message marked urgent. Sanaa chose that one.

Ms. Chase. I have called incessantly because I have great news. You have been chosen as Essence Magazine's Woman of the year In Business. The Trailblazer Award. Congratulations Ms. Chase! There's an award ceremony in two weeks, and the full article will run after that. We have lots to do with photo shoots and gown selection, so please call me when you get the message. I'm so happy for you!

Sanaa smiled. That was surprising and very unexpected news. "Essence Magazine, huh," she said aloud. As she started down the promenade toward baggage, Sanaa listened to her bestie's voicemail.

"Hey, girl. I'm not sure if you're still being held against your will or what but if you get back in time, the Moore girls are getting together for drinks at Kennedy's house Sunday afternoon. I know we usually do brunch at her restaurant, but we decided to hang at her place since she's getting so pregnant. Come through. I'll text you the address. Hope you're having the best time ever. Love you and be safe."

That sounded good to Sanaa. Although she could spend a leisurely afternoon at home, Sanaa knew herself better than that. It would be too quiet, and after a short nap, she would wake up and start thinking about work. And then Sanaa would be working.

"Not today," Sanaa smiled as she approached the baggage carousel. There was a car waiting for Sanaa when she exited the airport.

"Where to, Ms. Chase," the driver asked once he got Sanaa comfortable.

"5933 Wilmington Court," Sanaa replied. It was Kennedy's address.

Sᴀɴᴀᴀ ᴄᴏᴜʟᴅ ʜᴇᴀʀ ᴛʜᴇ ʟᴀᴜɢʜᴛᴇʀ ᴀs sʜᴇ ᴀᴘᴘʀᴏᴀᴄʜᴇᴅ ᴛʜᴇ house. The Moore women. Sanaa had a few occasions to be in their presence. Whether it was just a few of the women or all the Moore women, laughter was always present. Sanaa took a chance on ringing the doorbell, hoping someone would hear her. She had the driver stop before arriving to pick up a bottle of wine. Sanaa didn't want to show up empty-handed. Just as Sanaa got ready to ring the doorbell again, it swung open.

"Sanaa! So glad you're here," Aubrey, one of the younger Moore sisters said. "Come on in."

"It's been a while," Sanaa replied as she stepped over the threshold and extended a hug which Aubrey readily accepted.

"Too long," Aubrey smiled as they parted. "We're in the back."

This was the first time Sanaa had been to Kennedy's home. As she walked in pace with Aubrey Sanaa took note of how nice her place was. Although expansive, it was comfortable and felt homey. The ladies padded through to the back of the house where there was a luxurious four seasons room replete with fireplace, deep shag rugs covering the hardwood floors, and seating for all the Moore women who filled the space.

"Ladies, look who joined us?" Aubrey announced as they entered the room.

"Sanaa," several of the sisters and cousins chorused. Tempestt was the first on her feet as she approached Sanaa with her arms wide open.

"Hey everybody," Sanaa answered.

"Girl you are glowing about as much as Ken," Tempestt whispered as the friends hugged.

"What," Sanaa feigned ignorance.

"We'll talk about it later," Tempestt promised with a smile.

Kennedy was the next one to stand. Even though it took her a minute to lift her frame from the chair, Kennedy wore a beautiful smile as she padded towards Sanaa. Tempestt was right. Kennedy was absolutely radiant.

"Sanaa! It's so good to see you," Kennedy beamed.

"Kennedy, pregnancy looks good on you," Sanaa replied walking into the hug Kennedy offered her.

"Thanks, girl," Ken sighed as the two separated. "That is kind of you to say cause this baby is wearing me out."

"And your home, Kennedy, it's beautiful," Sanaa said as she followed Tempestt and Kennedy into the inner circle.

"That was all Bryce," Kennedy replied, slowly descending into the seat. "He didn't want me stressing out about the house and the baby coming, honey, so my amazing husband had crews working around the clock to get the house done."

"Well they did that," Sanaa smiled.

"They sure did," Daphne agreed. For many of the Moore girls, this was their first time seeing the finished product.

"We've got a few more things to do, but for the most part, it's done," Ken replied, rubbing her protruding belly.

"Do you know whether you're having a boy or a girl," Sanaa asked, as she sat down on the sofa next to Tempestt and Emery.

"The women in this room are not having it," Kennedy huffed.

"We sho'll ain't," Ivory chided, and Persia agreed.

"They are a mess, girl," Kennedy laughed.

"We are having a gender reveal party," Ivory continued. "And you're all invited. Bryce is on board. Kennedy just has to get there."

"That sounds like fun," Samantha added.

"It's like a whole thing," Kennedy sighed. "I have no idea how they are going to pull this off, but they even have mom and dad all excited."

"We got this covered," Ivory reminded. "Don't worry your pretty little head about it."

"I won't," Kennedy smiled. "But right now, your niece or nephew or both are hungry."

"I'll get you a plate," Felicity replied as she got up from the chair.

"Sanaa, get you a plate too. There's plenty of food," Kennedy added.

"Anytime Kennedy is around. There is always food, Charity added. "Between Ken and Bryce, we all are going to have to step up our exercise game."

"Congratulations are in order I understand, Charity," Sanaa offered.

"Yes, girl thank you," Charity beamed casting her eyes down to her wedding rings.

"Girl she is under the O'Shea spell," Tempestt laughed.

"Have you seen him?" Charity laughed. "Don't answer that!" Charity playfully clapped back. "Mrs. Malone."

"Eww, yass, girl," Tempestt smiled with two snaps of her finger. "I love the way that sounds."

Several of the girls took to the food spread that Ken and Bryce laid out for them. Sanaa didn't even realize how hungry she was until her stomach started growling as her eyes drank in the food in front of her. It was classic L'Arbre; shrimp etouffee, red beans, and rice, muffulettas fish Po-boys, fresh vegetable and fruit, and for dessert, beignets and bananas foster.

"I see what you mean about upping the exercise plan," Sanaa smiled as she fixed her plate.

"I told you," Charity smiled. "But don't skimp because we can work out later."

Sanaa's stomach rumbled again. "I don't plan to."

Everyone gathered in the seating area and enjoyed talking and great food.

"Okay ladies," Emery announced. "Who has good news to share?"

"Well," Daphne began. "I have a bit of good news," she began.

"Do tell, sister, do tell," Felicity encouraged.

"Things have gone exceptionally well at my school," Daphne began. "And I am happy to announce that we are opening a second school. We will have a second Moore Academy for Girls. This is more than about me; no pun intended," Daphne continued. "This is about our family legacy."

"That's amazing, Daphne," Trinity replied.

"You go then headmistress," Samantha agreed.

"Where's the new school going to be," Persia asked.

"Well," Daphne sang.

Uh oh," Aubrey sighed. "I don't like the way that sounded."

"What's up?" Emery asked, her curiosity piqued as well.

"Spill it," Ivory encouraged. "Cause that well was kind of ugh."

"Where's the second school, Daphne," Trinity echoed.

"Rural Ghana," Daphne finally answered.

"Ghana?" Emery asked.

The room fell silent, which was a feat considering all the women loved conversing.

"Let me explain," Daphne began. "You know my husband's company is international. We had a chance to visit Ghana on one of his late trips last year. I was enamored; moved by the culture and the people and especially the girls. Their eyes were bright, and their minds were brighter. What some of us would see as an undeveloped country and culture, these girls saw the beauty and possibilities in their everyday circumstances; some of which unpolluted by westernized thoughts and appropriation. The ingenious way in which they bridged the gap from technology to work the land, making it bountiful; that feeling didn't leave me when I left," Daphne swelled, placing a hand over her heart. "Nicholas saw how moved I was. We talked about it, and we talked about the ideas I had. And like my amazing husband, he was behind me 100%. So, a new school in Ghana. Now, in the initial stages I will have to spend a lot of time there, you know, getting things established. But you all have passports, right? And if you don't, you need to get them because I want everyone who can come to visit, especially for the grand opening!"

"That is so awesome," Charity replied. "Anything I can do to help, you already know."

"Congrats again," Daphne. "That is fantastic," Samantha replied.

"I think it's great, too," Aubrey added. "And I'm all for it. I will do whatever I can to help. But, you couldn't build a second school in, I don't know, Alpharetta? Palmetto? Hell, somewhere in the United States," Aubrey asked.

"Aw, Aubrey, I'm gonna miss you, too, but I won't be gone forever," Daphne said with a downturn of her lips. Although all the sisters were close, Aubrey and Daphne were particularly close. They'd always been. They were kindred in that way.

"I know," Aubrey pouted. "But I don't have to like it."

"We'll be here for you, girl," Charity smiled.

"I know, Aubrey answered. "I just want everybody to stay close, you know? We're sisters, cousins, friends. We're family. And even though everybody is getting married up and having beautiful babies, we are all we got."

"Now, you're making me sad and sentimental," Kennedy sighed. "And I'm already hormonal."

There were sighs all around.

"Let me say something," Samantha interjected. "As the oldest Moore girl, but the newest," Samantha smiled, receiving all smiles in return, "This family, no matter how it grows, has enough love to cover thousands and thousands of miles."

"That is so true," Kennedy sighed as a single tear fell onto her rosy cheek.

Aw, come on now, Ken," Emery whined. "If you start crying, then we'll all be crying. It's contagious."

"I know girl, but I can't help it," Kennedy continued as another tear fell. "That was one of the sweetest things I ever heard."

"Thanks, Sam," Aubrey answered, wiping a tear of her own.

Even Sanaa felt her eyes mist over. Her family was nothing like this one, nothing. She got a glimpse of what sisterly love was like with Tempestt. But this unconditional love between all these women connected by more than blood? Sanaa had no idea this kind of family, this kind of love even existed. Sure, fairy tales and lifetime movies suggested it was possible, but she had never witnessed family like this in real life. Sanaa was more than touched. The feeling made her think about Kingston.

"Is that a tear I see," Tempestt asked quietly, nudging her shoulder to Sanaa's.

"Maybe," Sanaa whispered, her eyes trailing to the blazing fire that certainly reminded her of the nights she spent in Colorado. "It's so pathetic," Sanaa sighed.

"The D was that good, huh," Tempestt taunted.

"Mmhmm," Sanaa giggled.

"Aw my damn," Tempestt giggled, covering her mouth with her hand.

"What are you two going on about?" Persia asked leaning in.

"Nothing," Sanaa quickly quipped.

"Mmhmm," Felicity snided.

"Sounds like something to me," Trinity added.

"Well," Tempestt began, giving Sanaa another nudge on the shoulder.

"Don't you dare," Sanaa insisted, pushing back against Tempestt. Sanaa didn't have to share about herself with family. She didn't really have one to speak of. When she did meet Tempestt, and the whole concept of girlfriends sharing their innermost thoughts and secrets came up, Sanaa didn't know how or if she trusted the process. She learned eventually, to open up to some degree about herself, however, Sanaa's go to had always been defense and guarded openness.

"Spill Tempestt or Sanaa," Trinity encouraged.

"It's nothing," Sanaa offered.

"Nobody believes it at this point," Felicity suggested.

"She's going to kill me later, Tempestt began, standing up to get out of Sanaa's striking range. "But my girl has a new boo, and he is Tempestt approved honey!"

Girl, that's nothing to whisper about," Trinity sang. "That's something you shout about, especially if he is Tempestt approved, which means, he is a good guy."

Sanaa's cheeks flushed. She was genuinely embarrassed. The other women in the room noticed it.

"What's the matter, Sanaa," Sam asked, recognizing that look because she'd worn one similar.

"Nothing, Sanaa quipped, looking away and refusing to make eye contact with anyone. Intellectually she understood that her avoidance only made the situation more intriguing but, in this instance, Sanaa couldn't help it.

"The one thing I know about these women in this circle is that you are safe here," Samantha reassured. "Good, bad or indifferent, you can share here. They will cheer with you, cuss with you, cry with you, but at all times, look out for you. Trust me. I wasn't one of those kinds of people who opened up, but that didn't stop the Moore women, chile. They let me have it when I needed it and supported me when I didn't even realize I needed that too," Sam continued.

Tempestt moved back to her seat next to Sanaa. She could see her friend squirming, and that wasn't her intention. Still, somehow Tempestt hoped Sanaa would take away the good from this situation. She knew personally how much the support of the group meant to her. Sanaa sat quietly, hearing what Samantha had to say and the words of support and encouragement from the other women. Sanaa looked around the room at the women sitting in the circle. Some she had met before, some she was just meeting. What Sanaa didn't feel was competition between the women, jealousy or anything of the sort. What she saw and what she felt was that these women really cared about each other. She shook her head in disbelief. Just like back at Kingston's, Sanaa felt like the food must have been spiked with truth serum. Against her historical judgment, Sanaa decided to respond.

"I'm not used to this," Sanaa began. "And," Sanaa paused. "I don't know if I can trust what I'm feeling."

"Sanaa, we are all women; women who have been there done that. Even if it's not the same thing, trust and believe we have all struggled with whether the 'he' in our lives or new to our lives is the right one," Emery suggested.

"Can I get an amen?" Kennedy asked, waving her hand in the air like she was in Sunday morning service.

There was a resounding chorus of amens and 'I know that's right,' from the women around Sanaa.

The sound of women who understood made Sanaa smile and relaxed a little. Tempestt was right there with her, leaning in; this time, not in jest, but to remind Sanaa that she was a shoulder to lean on.

"Maybe it would be helpful if Tempestt tells us why this man meets her approval? Aubrey suggested.

"That's a great idea, Aubrey," Tempestt replied, turning to Sanaa and smiling. "It's easy, actually," Tempestt continued. "This young man is intelligent. That's important because Sanaa would run psychological circles around an unintelligent man. He is also business savvy and has the kind of business accouterment that appeals to her. More importantly, he is persistent, not easily distracted from his goals, and strong-willed. Would you say that was accurate, Sanaa?"

Sanaa rolled her eyes. "did you say he was a pest, a kidnapper and hard-headed?"

"What?" Felicity asked. "Kidnapper? You're gonna have to explain that one!"

"Seriously," Charity agreed.

With much exaggeration, Tempestt whipped around to Sanaa. She couldn't wait to hear Sanaa tell the story.

"Did ya'll miss the pest and hard-headed part?"

"Nope, didn't miss it," Emery replied. "Just not as interested."

There were agreements from many of the women in the group; much to Sanaa's dismay. Sanaa threw a casually dismissive hand in Emery's direction and noticed that they were waiting for her to explain.

"Fine," Sanaa quipped. "This man went so far as to contact my boss on a business trip requesting my specific services. Cool. The company does business with this man, I handle his account, okay. But and that but is a big but, he had ulterior motives that had nothing to do with his account."

"That sounds like creativity and persistence to me, chile. What's the problem?" Ivory snapped.

"For real, girl! Whisk me away on some undercover personal agenda," Daphne added. Again, there was amens and agreement all around her. Noticing the upturn to Sanaa's lip Samantha waited until the side conversations died down before interjecting.

"What's the problem, Sanaa?" Sam asked.

"The problem?" Sanaa repeated. "It was false pretenses, gamey. I felt duped! And it was in Colorado in the cold and snow!" Sanaa crossed her arms over her chest to add emphasis to the point she was making. Internally, she rolled her eyes at her own actions. She sounded like a spoiled brat having a tantrum. Still, that's how she felt. They laughed at her response and Sanaa found herself smiling too, even though she still tried to maintain a hard exterior.

"That's not the problem, though," Samantha answered; not engaging in the frivolity and her eyes never leaving Sanaa. The rest of the women quieted down hearing the tone of Sam's response. Now, Sanaa felt all their eyes on her as well in expectancy. She sighed, breathing out low and slow. She knew that Sam saw through the bravado and sought to get to the heart of the matter.

"I don't trust it. I can't."

"Why?" Sam was direct. She made Sanaa feel like they were the only two people in the room.

"Because," Sanaa chimed.

"Okay," Samantha answered. "Had he told you what he really wanted, would you have gone?"

"No," Sanaa admitted.

"Because?" Now it was Sam's turn to ask the single word question.

"I just told you, I don't trust like that."

"That may be true, but that's not all of it."

"I like to be in control. That's important to me." Sanaa owned her response because it was the truth.

"Has he given you a reason not to trust him?"

Sanaa shrugged her shoulders and shook her head.

"So, the trust issues and the control issue are all you, is that right?" Sam continued.

"Pretty much," Sanaa replied.

"In other words, had this young man not gone through the antics and deception as you describe it you wouldn't have gone or discovered that there was something between you. Is that right?" Kennedy asked.

Sanaa's lack of response was admission enough.

"He sounds like exactly what you need," Samantha

replied. She saw Sanaa's eyebrow pitch but didn't allow that to dissuade her from what she had to say. "Trust, especially with a man, was hard for me, too. I needed the control because of my inability to trust. So, I get it, Sanaa. I get that you feel the need to protect yourself. I did too."

"And I understand why this man is Tempestt approved. He is persistent, pushing past your pain control issues, and insecurities because he knows exactly what he wants," Emery added.

"He sees you," Tempestt offered.

"And that's a good thing!" Aubrey chimed.

"That's the best thing," Felicity commented.

"Ugh," Sanaa moaned. She felt so many things being with Kingston that were brand new to her.

"Listen," Kennedy began as she rubbed the swell of her belly. "And this is for all of us, so Sanaa doesn't feel like she's being singled out. Love is messy and frightening and unnerving. Love throws you off balance and makes you question a whole lot of things, even yourself. But it's also life, and life-affirming, and enjoyable especially with the right one. Trust yourself. Trust that your truest self knows what you need even if the self that you show the world is unsure. Trust yourself, and then you can trust him. Then you won't have to control everything. Submission to what your heart feels, submission to the right man who has a vision for your lives together is a relief. It is not a burden."

"That thing preached itself," Persia sang.

"Pass the offering plate cause that's a whole sermon," Trinity agreed.

"And let that man love you Sanaa. I agree with Tempestt. Ladies, is this man Moore girl approved?"

"Yes, he is!" They agreed.

"I just want to know one thing," Daphne interjected. "Does this man have a name?"

Sanaa flushed. She could see him weaning a brooding

smile. She could feel his eyes drinking her in and his hands holding her close.

"Yes," Sanaa smiled. "His name is Kingston."

"Ah, come on now! Kingston, baby!" Ivory sang.

"Yes, hunty, the king!" Daphne laughed.

Sanaa blushed even harder. They celebrated him. They celebrated her struggle with letting him in, but they celebrated, nonetheless. She didn't feel chastised by the conversation. It was clarifying and uplifting. Sanaa was glad she came.

Chapter Fourteen

*T*hat night, after spending a wonderful evening with the Moore women, Sanaa got a phone call. She smiled as soon as she saw his name light up her phone screen.

"Were your ears burning," Sanaa asked a sheepish grin spread across her lips. Kingston was familiar with the phrase.

"Were you talking about me or thinking about me," his seductive voice crooned through the phone.

"You want a confession," Sanaa smiled.

"You just did," Kingston grinned.

"Whatever!"

"But, you're not confessing alone, Kingston answered.

"What does that mean?" The smile Sanaa wore couldn't be erased. She was smiling from the inside, and that was foreign.

"That your ears should've been burning, too," Kingston admitted.

"Oh, so were you talking about me or thinking about me," Sanaa flushed.

"Both," Kingston chortled. "That's why I'm here."

"Wh- What," Sanaa asked, sitting bolt upright in her bed. "What do you mean here? Atlanta?"

"No, beautiful," Kingston smirked. "Look outside your window."

Slowly, Sanaa's eyes traipsed to her bedroom window. "How did you even know where I live? Never mind," Sanaa huffed. "You are a resourceful man. But what in the world are you doing here?"

"I couldn't stop thinking about you," Kingston replied with no hesitation. "I missed you as soon as you left. Kingston laughed. "I even found myself talking to Zeus about you, even though I knew he couldn't respond. I think he misses you, too."

Her cheeks warmed as Sanaa's face flushed. She missed Kingston, too; a nascent feeling that Sanaa never experienced before. Sanaa lifted from her bed and slowly padded to her bedroom window. She stood out of eyesight as she eased the curtain back; just enough to see the street below. There Kingston was, in all his fine handsome glory, leaning against his car and looking up at her window. Even from this distance, Sanaa felt like Kingston's eyes found her and penetrated her gaze. She missed him. No man ever had that kind of effect on Sanaa before. She ever allowed it. This feeling of missing someone didn't even apply to Sanaa's family. She never missed them. There was nothing but pain to miss. At first, the feeling was hard to identify; the fluttering in the stomach, the constant present and fleeting thoughts, the ache. That's what missing someone felt like and admittedly, Sanaa missed Kingston.

"What are you doing here?" Sanaa asked as her finger slowly railed across her chin as she kept her eyes on Kingston.

"I just told you, Sanaa, I missed you."

"You could have called?" She teased.

"I could have," Kingston agreed. "But that only would have made me miss you more. I don't think my heart could take that."

"Your heart?"

"Yes, my heart, beautiful," Kingston crooned. "It aches for you."

"Oh really?"

"Yes," Kingston answered. "I see you still don't believe me."

"It's not that," Sanaa sighed. "I just don't understand."

"That's fair," Kingston replied. "But what about my aching heart?"

"What about it?"

"I need to see you, to stop my heart from aching."

"Now?"

"Yes, beautiful, now."

Sanaa fingered her silk scarf and looked down at what she was wearing.

"I'm not dressed," Sanaa replied.

"You forget," Kingston chortled. "I've seen you."

"True," Sanaa laughed. "Fine, King. Give me fifteen minutes."

"Fifteen minutes and not one minute more. Don't leave me in pain."

Sanaa disconnected the line and released the curtain before crossing the bedroom to the bathroom. She turned on the light and made her way to the mirror. Sanaa removed the silk wrap she wore and finger-fluffed her tresses. Any other time Sanaa wouldn't even entertain the compunctions of a man. She would have verbally chastised the guy for being presumptuous and inappropriate. Sanaa would have ensured the man felt small and apologetic when she was done with him. But this was not any man. This was Kingston Wells, the man who seemed determined to woo her and win Sanaa's heart no matter how hard she fought against it. There was a part of Sanaa that wanted to look her best, even if it was in the middle of the night with an unsolicited visitor. But Kingston reminded Sanaa that he'd seen her. There was no need to spruce up. If Kingston thought he desired her, she would let him see her just as she was.

Exiting the bathroom, Sanaa turned off the light and traipsed through her bedroom, down the stairs to the front door. Taking a deep breath and fingering her hair once again, Sanaa opened the door. She felt Kingston's eyes find her. Sanaa felt a fluttering of her heart too; a wrenching in her gut and a rush of adrenaline pulse through her. Sanaa waited a beat and tried to level her breathing. She didn't want to appear anxious or excited. The old Sanaa was still there, lurking in the shadows, insisting that she played it cool. Once accomplished, Sanaa descended the stairs and slowly sashayed in Kingston's direction. Even though she tried to be cool, a smile eased across her lips as Kingston moved towards her.

"Hey beautiful," Kingston sighed as he closed the last remaining distance between them. Sanaa didn't have a chance to respond though. Kingston swept her up in his arms and leveled Sanaa with a passionately delicious kiss. Instantly, she melded into his strong, embracing arms. There was safety and sanctity in the way Kingston held her. His lips caressed hers, and Kingston's tongue coaxed Sanaa to kiss him deeper. She felt completely weightless in Kingston's arms. The swoon in her spirit and the churn in her gut snatched the remaining air from Sanaa's lungs as she tried to regain that same air into her depleted yet pounding chest. Her eyes fluttered open as Kingston eased his lips away from her but not without leaving a lasting feathery kiss for Sanaa to remember.

"Hey," Sanaa flushed.

Kingston's returned smile was partially covered by his hand as he lightly stroked his chin.

"I can't believe you are standing outside my house."

"Not sure why that is, since I told you," Kingston chortled.

"I know what you said, Kingston," Sanaa replied.

"But you still have a hard time believing that I find you incredibly irresistible? Is that it, beautiful?"

Sanaa laughed. "And I don't know why it's so hard considering I consider myself incredibly irresistible." *Or I did before you* is the part Sanaa didn't say aloud. Kingston unnerved every part of Sanaa while building her up and boosting her. The contradiction is what kept Sanaa feeling off kilter when she was around him.

"That's the Sanaa I saw the first time we met," Kingston laughed, "feisty, confident, cocky even."

"Be careful," Sanaa warned. "She's still here."

"She better be," Kingston crooned.

The two fell silent as they both repositioned themselves leaning against Kingston's car, side by side. The street was quiet except for the occasional distant sound of a car passing. The sky was dark in some areas and sprinkled with shiny stars in others. There wasn't really a breeze to speak of, but the temperature was nice; not too hot and not too cold. More than that, it was nice just being with Sanaa. She felt the same. It was nice just being with Kingston.

"We have a choice to make, beautiful," Kingston began, breaking the pleasantness of the silence.

"And what choice is that?"

"Well, I can be satisfied having seen you and having the taste of your seductive lips linger on my mouth," Kingston began.

"Or?" Sanaa said flirtatiously.

"Or, we can continue what we started in Colorado, but this time on your own turf."

"What? Having mind-altering sex," Sanaa purred.

"That too, Kingston laughed. "But I was referring to getting to know each other better."

"Oh," Sanaa sighed and then smiled.

Kingston moved closer to Sanaa until their bodies connected, although they still remained next to each other.

He leaned in, his lips close to Sanaa's ear.

"And if we happen to have mind-altering sex too, then," Kingston whispered.

"Then what?" Sanaa laughed.

"Then I am all for it."

"I bet you would be," Sanaa sang.

When Kingston moved in front of her, Sanaa didn't know what to make of it. When she looked up into his handsome face, she saw Kingston's brow furrowed and his dark eyes piercing.

"Let's be clear," Kingston commanded, not only with his presence but with the baritone of his voice. Sanaa continued to look up into Kingston's eyes, transfixed by him. "Being with you is more than sex. And I need you not just to hear me but feel what I'm saying beautiful. Don't reduce it to just that. Sex is great," Kingston continued. "But it's not everything, not for me, not with you. Your connection is what I crave. Feeling your heart beat next to mine is what I desire."

Sanaa's fingers meandered up Kingston's shirt, landing just short of the top button.

"Hush, King," Sanaa insisted as her finger found its way to Kingston's lips. "You had me at let's be clear."

They both smiled, yet there was something underneath the smiles that was alluring. She saw it in Kingston's eyes. He saw it in hers. Sanaa's hand moved down Kingston's chest to his hand hanging by his side. Kingston folded his hand into Sanaa's, and he willingly followed as Sanaa led him into her home.

"Very nice," Kingston commented as they crossed the threshold. "I can see you everywhere."

"How's that," Sanaa asked. Kingston closed the door behind them and turned the top lock. He followed Sanaa into the living room where she extended a hand for him to sit.

Kingston's eyes trailed across Sanaa's space as she sat down next to him. "I can see you reflected everywhere; parts of your personality, those you willingly share and those you try to hide."

"Wait one minute," Sanaa insisted; her hand sliding up the curve of her hip until it rested comfortably on her waist. "I want to hear this, but first, let me get something for us to drink. Deal?"

"Deal," Kingston agreed with a chuckle.

Spinning on her heels, Sanaa made her way into the kitchen, returning with a bottle of Riesling and two wine goblets on a silver tray. She made Kingston hold his thoughts until they both had half-filled goblets in their hands and Sanaa was comfortable on the couch having kicked off her shoes and tucking her feet underneath.

"Okay, now go," Sanaa suggested as she took a sip of the wine.

"Well," Kingston began, "there is an interest yet subtle theme that runs through your décor. There are strong straight lines like the chrome rods at the windows, and the brushed chrome trim of the tables and dining room chairs positioned against deep colors in soft fabrics."

"And what pray tell do you draw from that, Mr. Wells?" Sanaa asked intrigued.

"The straight lines are metal demonstrating strength. What I read Ms. Chase is the extroverted strength you show the world in the chrome and the quieter strength like the brushed silver that you carry inside."

"Mmhmm," Sanaa purred. "And the deep colors?"

"That's easy," Kingston smiled; casually holding the glass in his hand. "The colors, the eggplant, the smoky grays, the dark greens are a reflection of the complexities of your personality, deep thoughts, deep thinking, deep feelings."

"Aha," Sanaa grinned. "Anything else from this appraisal?"

"Just one other thing," Kingston replied, turning his full attention to Sanaa.

"And what is that?"

"There are light, soft details that catch the eye as you look around. It would be easy to see the strong decorative statements and miss the more subtle softer ones."

"And what do you think that says about me?"

"That the softer sides of you aren't obvious unless you take the time to look."

"You think you know me so well," Sanaa quipped.

"Am I wrong?" Kingston asked, taking a sip from his glass.

Pouting her lips and tilting her head slightly, Sanaa gave her answer. "No."

"And still, beautiful, there is so much more I want to know."

"You know so much already," Sanaa replied, adjusting on the couch. "What else is there?"

Kingston reached out rubbing Sanaa's shoulder before resting his arm on the back of the couch. "What makes your eyes so sad. That's what I want to know," Kingston answered. "It's not all the time," he clarified, "but there are moments when things are quiet, and you don't think anyone is paying attention that I see it, such incredible sadness."

Kingston was not surprised when Sanaa fell silent. She turned slightly away from him and took the last sip from her goblet. Although she was cognizant of Kingston's observation, she couldn't keep the sadness from creeping back into her gaze.

"I don't want to talk about the sadness," Sanaa quietly rebuffed. Her eyes turned away again, avoiding contact with Kingston although his eyes never left her. Kingston didn't press, and then Sanaa spoke again. "Did you know I won an award? Trailblazer award from Essence."

"That's wonderful, Sanaa. You are so deserving," Kingston iterated.

"Thanks," Sanaa sighed with a slight upturn of her lips.

"So, no talk of sadness, not tonight or this morning or whatever it is, okay?"

Her eyes found Kingston again. Sanaa needed him to understand everything she said and what she didn't. There was a pleading in her eyes that surpassed the sadness. Kingston sat forward on the couch and picked up the bottle of wine; filling first Sanaa's glass and then his own. Sitting the bottle back on the table, Kingston sat closer to Sanaa.

"Let's toast to your well-deserved award. No more talk of sadness," Kingston offered. Relieved, Sanaa lifted her glass in response to Kingston and clicked them, taking a hefty sip. Kingston's intention was not to bring down the mood. But he could see that's exactly what his last observation had done. He wanted to make up for that.

"Come here, beautiful," Kingston encouraged, reaching for Sanaa. Their eyes connected and she saw his concern. Sanaa sat her glass on the table and moved into Kingston's open arms.

"I didn't mean to push, beautiful," Kingston whispered against her ear. "When I see the sadness, though, I want to do something about it, to erase it, to make things better because I care just that much. I never want you sad, Sanaa."

"I feel that," Sanaa sighed; nodding as she spoke.

Sanaa stood to her feet and then turned and extended her hand to Kingston. He accepted and lifted his frame to her. He followed as Sanaa padded across the living room, down the hall, and into the master bedroom. Sanaa continued to hold Kingston's hand as she turned and backpedaled the last few steps into the master. The undressing was Kingston's gift to Sanaa. He was slow, patient, and removed his clothing as he removed hers. She tried to help, feeling pulsations rise in her gut that was hard to suppress.

"All I want you to do is stand here and take it," Kingston encouraged with a low guttural voice that was nearly an intense whisper. Their eyes met, connected, and his penetrated hers to the point that she felt the piercing through her soul.

"You make me sick," Sanaa moaned, rolling her eyes and trying to be cool.

"Take it," Kingston insisted.

The command from him is what she craved although before Sanaa would have resisted. When Kingston was finished, He stood naked before her, the sculpt of his muscle-toned body drawing in more than Sanaa's eyes. He left nothing for Sanaa to hide behind, to bravado behind. She stood naked before him as well.

Kingston cradled her, rocking her in the strength of who he was and who he desired to be in Sanaa's life. She willingly accepted him. Kingston enveloped her and pulled Sanaa in close, and they both moved towards the bed. Their mouths connected, first lightly, then deeply as he tasted her tongue while she tasted his. The heat in the room increased ten-fold as Kingston eased his hand high enough to feel Sanaa's mound. Kingston needed to taste more than her mouth; leaving a trail of tantalizing kisses from her lips, down her neck, and to her center. Sanaa moaned as her body responded to Kingston's masterful touch. Easing between her thighs, Kingston breathed in deeply, taking in her essence. The first kiss to her jewel sent a surge of heated energy to Sanaa's puss. She spread her legs wider for him, inviting Kingston to feast at her table.

Parting her lips with his fingers, Kingston plunged his thick, hot tongue inside her folds. Sanaa's back arched without prompting. He plunged deeper, filling her walls and flitting her throbbing clit. Kingston pulled away, separating his lips from her flesh and then blew softly. Sanaa quivered and clawed at the sheets beside her. When his mouth reconnected with her quaking jewel, Kingston lapped up the lovely juices Sanaa so freely gave. Intensifying the moment, Kingston inserted one finger, then another; driving deep inside her.

"Oh, King," Sanaa whimpered.

As his hardness grew, Kingston's finger-fuck intensified. Sanaa's nipples hardened as Kingston hit her g-spot over and over again. Unable to hold out any longer, Kingston slithered up the length of her; his dick finding her wet pussy waiting.

"Aw shit," he growled as the heat from her box met his thickness. Wrapping her legs around his strong back, Sanaa pulled Kingston in. They fell in sync as she moved her hips circularly filling her womanly walls. Kingston's dick throbbed. Sanaa offered new wetness coating him. He couldn't get enough of her, rocking Sanaa with his powerful thrusts. When she moaned again, Kingston eased her legs from around him and slid his hands down, cupping her ass. He lifted Sanaa slightly and lifted on his knees. The fuck came harder, faster as his sack slapped against Sanaa's plump ass. The sound of their bodies connecting and reconnecting as only matched by the moans and groans escaping their lips. The bed rocked under the thunder of Kingston's dick pushing the top of Sanaa's jewel.

Sanaa reached for him. But Kingston's stroke quickened. She fell back onto the bed, grabbing and gripping whatever her hands could hold.

"Kingston," she screamed as he leaned forward, lifting her higher and fucking her senseless. The pace was furious, and their bodies clapped together. Sanaa's thighs were wet with perspiration, and her eyes rolled inside her head as Kingston sent her on a wave of ecstasy.

"Cum with me, beautiful," he uttered as his body convulsed from the pressure building inside him. Sanaa was boiling over, no longer in control. There was a quickening deep in her loins. The headboard pounded against the wall as a sound, unlike anything she ever heard, poured from Kingston as he spilled hotness inside her. She matched him, coating his thickness with sweet sticky nectar. The surge of orgasm was mind-numbing. Spent, Kingston collapsed on top of her. Sanaa folded her arms around him. Their hearts continued to race as they basked in the moment.

THEY FELL ASLEEP IN EACH OTHER'S ARMS; BOTH SPENT FROM their passionate entanglement. But as his eyes opened and he felt Sanaa nestled safely in his arms, Kingston's desire for her grew and could not be contained. She was everything his heart desired, and Kingston felt as though he was becoming that for Sanaa. Instead of shaking her awake, Kingston wrapped his thickly corded arms tighter around her and planted long slow kisses to the nape of her neck. He could feel her heartbeat, and he heard the softest moan escape her lips. Kingston was Sanaa's security, and he felt that as she lay so peacefully next to him. The soft kisses intensified as his desire and growing love for her roused the deepest parts of him. Sanaa was no longer asleep; feeling Kingston's manhood rise behind her; pressed against her. Kingston layered his kisses on Sanaa's neck. She felt the fullness of his lips and the tease of his tongue as he trailed hot kisses the length of her neck onto her shoulders. Reaching a hand behind her, Sanaa pulled Kingston closer. She wanted no space between them.

Kingston left heated kisses there that sent shivers to Sanaa's core. She pushed back against the thickness of his manhood, as her nipples pulsed and swole. Sanaa moaned again, enticing Kingston. With ease, he slipped his boxer's down and released the pressure that held his hardness captive. Now, it was flesh against flesh; the roundness of Sanaa's ass against the fullness of Kingston's stiff dick. Sanaa pulled Kingston closer, inviting him in. With one hand he lifted her cheek and found the warmness that was her jewel. She was ready to receive him as his kisses had already created a conclave of moisture there. Sanaa's nectar coated his shaft as he eased deep inside her; feeling her walls envelop him, filling her up with his goodness.

It was the moan that oozed from Kingston's lips pressed close to her ear that sent a wave of desire coursing through her. Sanaa guided Kingston's hand to her breast, and he cupped the fullness, finding her swollen nipple and twirling it between his thumb and forefinger. The pressure, the pain felt sweet to Sanaa as she ground down on his swollen manhood. Kingston bit down on Sanaa's neck, shooting even more pleasurable pain to her core and she whimpered under his touch. They fell into a deep syncopated rhythm; his push against her push; his dick hitting the top of her womb. Her moans became pants that ricocheted within Kingston. He wanted to please her. Kingston held her firmly as he pushed inside her; the muscles of his thighs tightening with every stroke. She was open to him fully, and Kingston lavished in the hot nectar that spilled from her.

Releasing the fullness of her breasts, Kingston cupped Sanaa's ass, spreading her cheeks wider for maximum exposure. He leaned in hitting the puss at a new angle that thrilled Sanaa's g spot. The groan that rose in Kingston came from the deepest recesses of his loins as hot gism threatened to spill from him. But he didn't want the intensity of the fuck to end. He bit down again on her shoulder as he held himself; not ready to release inside her. He felt Sanaa's body quivering under his touch. Sanaa gasped for air; feeling herself full of the man she loved. His stroke quickened but remained steady. Kingston pulled Sanaa on top of him with one move; her back to his front; the curve of his magic stick held tightly by her womanhood. Sanaa held his thickness in place, never wanting to let go.

"Damn bae," he whimpered as Sanaa lifted from his chest.

He held her back as she positioned herself to ride out the rest of what Kingston had to offer. Her ample ass moved up and down as her pussy worked his pole to the hilt. She swirled her hips and bent Kingston to her will. Sanaa's breasts bounced as she fell into her own rhythm; pleasing herself with what Kingston offered her. He couldn't hold back anymore; lifting himself up to her down stroke. Kingston held Sanaa's waist tight as he pounded her flesh. She squealed with delight as her pour met his pour until there was nothing left to give.

Sanaa's body glistened with sweat, but she held Kingston firmly inside her until he softened. It was only then that Sanaa leaned back against him, and Kingston's arms found her again. He wrapped his arms around her and held Sanaa close.

"Good morning…"

Chapter Fifteen

TWO WEEKS LATER

"$\mathcal{T}$hanks for being here with me," Sanaa whispered into Kingston's bent ear as they stood on the red carpet for the Woman of the Year Award.

"Thanks for wanting me here," Kingston whispered back as multiple cameras flashed, capturing the closeness of the couple on the carpet. Kingston and Sanaa shared an award-winning smile between them, and the paparazzi ate it up. The flashes intensified, and the calls from the cameramen increased. They called Sanaa's name, asked if they were a couple, and asked for more shots. Kingston stood proudly next to Sanaa and shared the spotlight with her. And then like the perfect gentleman he was, Kingston kissed Sanaa on the cheek and took a few steps back, giving Sanaa her time alone to shine for the world to see. She was resplendent in a form-fitting lavender gown, with drop sleeves exposing the cocoa of Sanaa's shoulders and a thigh-high split that provided a sneak peek at her luscious legs. The interspersed rhinestones sewn throughout the gown caught the light just right, softly sparkling as Sanaa moved. She wore her hair upswept with her ears adorned in platinum earrings with a one-carat diamond that glimmered. Strappy rhinestone studded four-inch Christian Louboutin's held Sanaa's pedicured feet and Kingston drank in her beauty with his brooding, appreciative gaze that the cameras did not miss.

Sanaa glanced down and smiled at the four-carat diamond bangle bracelet Kingston gave her as a congratulatory gift before looking over her shoulder, beckoning Kingston to her. The gift was unexpected and made Sanaa flush, even as she gazed upon on it this time. Kingston's response was swaggalicious as he stepped to her responding without hesitation, positioning himself on her side and raising his arm to escort her down the red carpet. The cameras never stopped flashing until the couple was inside the building. Kingston didn't let Sanaa go until they were in their seats, and even then, he held her hand and escorted the honoree to the podium when her name was called. Kingston returned to his seat as the applause for Sanaa continued and echoed around the theatre filled with people.

Sanaa smiled and flushed as those in the audience showed their appreciation for the woman of the year. "Thank you, thank you, everyone," Sanaa said as the applause began to die down. She had their full attention; none more than Kingston who looked at her with such pride in his eyes.

"Thank you to the Essence family for this incredible honor. Woman of the year? That's amazing. I don't think anyone; any woman does her job daily thinking there would be a tangible award for her labor. We, especially women, do our jobs, we labor because we are passionate and dedicated. We work for the desired outcome whether there is an acknowledgment of any kind, a pat on the back, a raise, anything. We do it because that's who we are. We are women; women doing business. Essence, you have taken the work that I do every day and acknowledged it. That means so much to me. But I do not accept this honor without acknowledging the work and the women whose shoulders I humbly stand upon. Those women who paved the way when paving the way wasn't easy so the little girl I used to be could dare to dream; could dare to become a woman who stands toe to toe with the men who have run business in this country since the beginning. There would be no me without those women, and for that, for this honor, I say thank you."

As Kingston stood to his feet, so did the rest of the audience with resounding applause for Sanaa. He stood at the bottom of the stairs and extended his hand to ensure she descended safely. Kingston's hand fell to the center of Sanaa's back as he moved with her to their seats.

"You were amazing," Kingston said as they sat down. "Simply amazing."

Sanaa flushed again and smiled a thank you to Kingston. When the presentations were over the cameras flashed just as brilliantly upon their exit as Kingston whisked her into the back of a chauffeured Bentley. Once settled, Sanaa turned her phone back on. Instantly, it began to beep and buzz with notifications, text messages and an incoming call.

"How dare you not tell me?"

"I have no excuse. Surprise?" Sanaa replied.

"I am your best friend; at least I thought I was," Tempestt fussed. "And I have to find out on social media and confirm on the news that my best friend received the Woman of the Year Award?"

"I'm sorry Tempestt," Sanaa explained. "Things have been so crazy these past few weeks, and you are my best friend, that will never change. I know that's not sufficient but, I am sorry."

"I forgive you," Tempestt sighed and then smiled. "I can't be too mad at you. Congratulations girl! That is so awesome and well deserved."

"Thanks, Tempestt, you know I appreciate you, Sanaa sighed, relieved that her best friend wasn't as upset as she could be.

"And you and Kingston on that red carpet?!? You two were the bomb! You guys looked incredible together!"

"Thank you," Sanaa smiled. She looked over her shoulder at Kingston who overheard Tempestt's jubilance. "Kingston said thank you, too," Sanaa giggled.

"You're with him right now?" Tempestt asked trying to whisper through her own giggles.

"Yes, I am," Sanaa smiled as Kingston stroked her hand.

"Squee! Okay, that's good," Tempestt swooned. "I'll talk to you later, and we can celebrate! Love you! Bye."

"Bye, Tempestt," Sanaa replied and disconnected the line.

"She's a good friend," Kingston observed as he pulled Sanaa into him.

"Yes, she is," Sanaa smiled. She found herself smiling a lot this evening, and not just because of the award. When Sanaa's phone rang again, she didn't bother looking at the caller ID figuring it was Tempestt calling back forgetting something or Chauncey updating her on the schedule.

"Hello," Sanaa sang into the phone.

There was no immediate reply. Sanaa could hear the line open and someone breathing on the other end, but that person didn't immediately respond.

"Hello?"

Kingston looked warily at Sanaa. She shrugged her shoulders considering hanging up. She paused long enough to pull the phone from her ear and see that the caller ID indicated unknown.

"No one on the other end," Kingston asked. Sanaa listened in still hearing the breathing, but the caller said nothing. Sanaa said hello again and then she heard the person clear their throat.

"Sanaa?"

"Yes, this is Sanaa. Can I help you?"

"Sanaa, it's me, baby."

Sanaa paused. Her eyes moved from side to side as her mind tried to figure it out.

"Sanaa, are you there? It's me. It's momma."

She froze, unable to think or move. The voice registered finally; a voice she hadn't heard in years. She didn't know what to say, what to think, how to respond. Sanaa's mother, Doris, had her daughter's number for a while. She secured it after some hunting; finding a business card with Sanaa's number on it. Doris had been tempted to call the number before, to reach out to her only child that she hadn't spoken with in years. She missed Sanaa. Although Doris took some responsibility for why there had been such distance, there was a part of Doris that refused to acknowledge and accept her failing as a parent; as a mother. She had moments, though, on both sides of the argument. Doris yearned to believe that the man she gave her life to, whether he deserved it or not, could not have done something so ghastly as to assault her daughter. She had to believe that at his core, he was better than that and maybe her daughter made up the allegation for attention. Doris was still with him. She still loved him. Maybe Doris had given too much attention to him and not her own child? Still, even after all these years, Doris figured it couldn't be true, and Sanaa blew things out of proportion as a child would. Doris missed so much of Sanaa's life. She missed her child. Maybe, Sanaa missed her too and was willing to let bygones be bygones?

"Why are you calling me," Sanaa stuttered into the phone, still unable to wrap her mind around what was going on.

"Because, baby, I saw you on television winning that award. You look so beautiful."

"Why are you calling me," Sanaa repeated in utter disbelief. Her heart sank in her chest, and her palms started to sweat. Her mothers was a voice she hadn't heard in years.

"I can see you've done well for yourself."

Her mother waited to hear something from her daughter; something that resembled acceptance, forgiveness.

"I just wanted you to know that I am so proud of you," her mother continued.

Taking a deep breath, Sanaa centered her mind. There was a cadre of emotions welling up in her spirit nearly choking back her words. She wanted to yell, be angry, curse her mother out for having the audacity to call her at a time like this, at any time really.

"Are you still with him?" Sanaa hissed into the phone.

"What? Why is that important?"

"Are you still with him?" Sanaa demanded. "Answer me."

"Yes, but that's- "

"That's always the point! Don't ever call me again."

Sanaa didn't wait for a response. It was like a ghost from her sordid past coming out of a closet that was locked, double bolted, and forgotten about. She was literally shaking as her hand gripped the phone tighter. Kingston could feel Sanaa vibrating against him. Her breathing was labored, and her eyes were focused straight ahead. He didn't say anything. This was not the time. A single tear rolled down Sanaa's cheek. She wasn't sad, Sanaa was pissed. Even when the chauffeur pulled into Sanaa's driveway, her disposition had not changed. Kingston was willing to wait as long as it was neces- sary for Sanaa to be ready to get out of the car. The driver waited on standby as well. After a few moments, Sanaa turned to Kingston and indicated that she was ready. The driver opened the door after being signaled by Kingston and Kingston helped Sanaa out of the car. They walked side by side to Sanaa's front door, and Kingston helped her with the key, seeing how bad her hand shook. Kingston opened the door, and Sanaa stoically crossed the threshold. It was like the wind had been taken out of her sails. She'd been flying so high just moments before, and now, the sadness was there. It wasn't just confined to Sanaa's eyes. The sadness had infiltrated her person, making her slow and stoic and silent. Kingston helped Sanaa to the couch. She sat down hard, and her eyes stayed focused straight ahead. Her mouth was downturned, and Sanaa's brows were elevated like she was in a state of surprise.

After a few moments, Kingston leaned over and lifted Sanaa's legs onto his, causing her to shift on the couch. Gently, Kingston unstrapped Sanaa's shoes and removed them. He encouraged Sanaa to rest her back on the couch as he began gingerly massaging her feet.

"Wow," Sanaa mumbled. "Just wow," Sanaa sighed.

"Do you want to talk about it?"

Sanaa paused, blinking and then staring straight ahead again.

"I don't even know what to say."

Kingston continued to massage Sanaa's feet, caressing her.

"I can't believe she had the sheer audacity to call me. How did she even call me? Like where in the hell did she get my number from and then to call me after all these years? Oh, and she's proud of me. Tuh," Sanaa said; the words spilling out in starts and stops. Her eyes found Kingston's and then left him again.

"Is your phone number public?" Kingston asked.

"Not necessarily public," Sanaa responded. "But accessible."

"That makes sense," Kingston replied.

"What doesn't make sense is that she called me at all," Sanaa hissed. "It's not like she gives a fuck about me."

Kingston noticed that Sanaa never referred to her mother with terms of endearment or even her mother's name; just a pronoun, she.

Sanaa huffed and folded her arms across her chest. "Proud of me, huh, she doesn't even know me."

Sanaa closed her eyes, and again, Kingston saw tears begin to stain her cheeks. He reached for Sanaa, but instead of falling into his arms, she pulled away. He had no choice but to respect it.

"She doesn't know you?" He repeated.

"She never cared enough to know me," Sanaa insisted.

"Talk to me, beautiful."

There was a part of Sanaa that wanted to tell Kingston, to open up and pour her guts out; her guts, not her soul. Her soul had been vacated a long time ago as a direct result of what happened to her. She lifted her legs from Kingston's lap and planted them on the floor. Her head fell to her hands as she lifted her elbows onto her legs. She wrestled with the part of herself that demanded self-protection at all costs. But the burden she carried alone seemed so heavy. Her shoulders slumped from the weight of it all. Slowly, Sanaa lifted her head, and she turned to Kingston. His eyes were kind. She didn't see any judgment there.

"She never cared about me because she was too busy caring about him. She always put him first; catering to him even though he was hateful and good for nothing. She had a habit of leaving me alone with him. At first, it was just for short periods of the time when she ran to the store or whatever. I never liked being alone with him. I always asked could I go with her, but she didn't listen. She blew me off, saying it was no big deal. Even before I knew what could happen to me, something in my gut made me uncomfortable being around him, even when she was there."

Kingston didn't interfere. He sat there with Sanaa, being supportive but not intrusive. He didn't raise any questions. This was a time for Sanaa to say what she wanted, what she needed without interruption. Sanaa barely spoke above a whisper, yet her words came out like heated darts; hard to say, difficult to speak; yet torched with constrained emotion. She pressed forward though, despite how painful talking about the situation was.

"Maybe it was the way he looked at me, even when she

was right there. Even when the woman he claimed to love, the woman he was there to be with was right in front of him, I could feel his eyes on me, looking at me; not like a man looks at a little girl but more like a man looking at a woman. He looked at me like he looked at her. One day," Sanaa swallowed hard.

"One day when she was gone, he started staring at me like he'd done before. My skin started to crawl, and I left the living room and walked fast to my bedroom. I figured in my little brain that if I was out of sight, I would be out of mind. But he followed me. I heard his heavy boots behind me, and he followed me. I tried to hurry up and get to my bedroom and close the door but the faster I walked, the faster he walked. I started running. The hallway was short, but I ran anyway and grabbed my door as soon as I got into my room and tried to close it. But his big hand grabbed the door. I remember seeing the dirt under his fingernails as he stopped the door from closing. I was scared and started to back into my room. I looked around for a way to get away from him, but he was bigger than me, stronger than me."

"He told me not to yell because if I did, he would hurt me and her too. I was too scared to yell though. I couldn't speak at all. I was scared out of my mind. He walked over to where I was, towering over me, and smiling. He had a gold tooth in the front of his mouth that made the rest of his teeth look rotten. When he reached for me, I wanted to fight him. I wanted to hit him to keep him from touching me, but his hands were so big that when he held me, I couldn't move. He started saying nice things to me like he cared about me and how pretty I was. He backed me up to the bed and laid me down, and I asked him to let me go, but he said everything was going to be okay. All I had to do was relax. When he let one of my arms go, I tried to fight him, to scratch him, to get him away from me, but my little hits must not have hurt. It definitely didn't stop him. Before I knew it, his filthy fingers were down my pants. He shoved his grimy fingers inside me. It hurt so bad I started to cry. All I could think about was the dirt under his nails and how those filthy nails were inside me. He just shushed me and told me to relax, that it would be okay. I think I blanked out. My eyes were open, so I must have still been awake. There was a light in the middle of my ceiling, and I just kept staring at it. he took my pants off and then my panties. All I could do," Sanaa's voice broke.

She paused, doing her damnedest to hold back the tears. Kingston felt her pain in his heart. He felt a swarm of emotions just hearing Sanaa's horrible experience. He could only imagine and empathize with how she felt. Kingston had a strong desire to reach for Sanaa; to hold her and apologize for what happened. He didn't though. Kingston followed her lead. If she reached for him, he would be there. If she needed to lean on him, he would be there. If she didn't, Kingston would still be there.

"All I could do was stare at the ceiling and try to take my mind off what was happening to me. Then, I couldn't breathe; he was so heavy on top of me. I never felt pain like that before. I just kept staring at the ceiling praying that it would be over. When it finally was, I don't even think I realize it. He grunted, groaned, sweated on top of me. Then, he was gone. What's weird is, I still felt the weight of him on top of me even after he left. Maybe it was the pain in my heart, the hurt in my soul."

A tear fell from Kingston's eye. He didn't wipe it away.

Sanaa was wringing her hands, slow and hard. The tears in her eyes and on her cheeks continued to fall. She didn't bother to wipe them away.

"It took me a while to get up. I don't know how long, but it was a while. My legs hurt so bad. The room was kind of dark, so I didn't see the mess I made... there was blood."

That's when Sanaa broke and allowed the little girl inside to cry her eyes out. She reached for Kingston's hand, and he was there for her; to hold her hand when she needed him to. The sobs that poured from Sanaa wrenched at Kingston's soul, and he wept internally with her.

"I got up the nerve to talk to her; to tell her what he did to me. I didn't wait. I didn't pay attention to his threats. I went to her when he wasn't around and told her everything he did to me. And you know what she said? The woman that gave birth to me? The woman who out of everyone should have been there for me, you know what she said? She said that there was no way in hell that her man, her man would do that to me. She called me a liar to my face. She didn't believe me, her own child."

Sanaa did wipe her eyes, and her cheeks so that no more tears were there. Kingston could see Sanaa tensing her jaw; the muscle tensing and relaxing and then tensing again. The pain was still there, but there was also anger evidenced by Sanaa's furrowed brow.

"So, I left. I was young, barely a teenager but that didn't matter. I couldn't stay there anymore because I knew she wouldn't protect me. And now after all this time, she calls me out of the blue to tell me she is proud of me? She doesn't even know me."

Sanaa continued to hold Kingston's hand, even after she stopped speaking.

"Say something," Sanaa whispered and then smiled slightly.

Kingston inhaled and slowly released the breath. He covered Sanaa's hand with both of his and focused his full attention to her.

"If no one has said it to you before, I am so sorry."

Kingston's reply was sincere and consoled Sanaa more than he knew. Because she hadn't ever shared the fullness of what happened to her with anyone, no one had ever said they were sorry. The people who should have never did. To her surprise, Sanaa was willing in her head, her heart and her soul to accept Kingston's apology.

"I wish there was a way I could take the pain, the hurt from you," Kingston continued. "I wish I could make it all go away. I know that I can't. What I can do is love you through it. I love you, beautiful, before and now."

"I don't have the best foundation on which love can be built," Sanaa quietly admitted. She did turn to Kingston allowing their eyes to meet. His consistency in being there for her with words and deeds opened her heart to who he was and who he could be to her. "But, I am falling for you…"

Chapter Sixteen

ONE WEEK LATER

"*T*hat smile you're wearing is awfully big," Chauncey teased.

"Excuse me?" Sanaa stopped as the two walked down the main hallway of Pinnacle. The firm had just given Ms. Chase a celebratory luncheon not only for the work she had done with Kingston's company but also for the Woman of the Year award that was bringing in a flood of prospective new clients who all wanted Ms. Chase to represent their interests.

"You heard me," Chauncey grinned, "no disrespect of course."

"Mmhmm," Sanaa hummed. She couldn't be mad though, even as her face flushed from the comment. Sanaa was smiling. It was true. And, it had nothing to do with the luncheon or the accolades. The ladies continued to the elevator and down to the first floor. Chauncey's hands were full of flowers and the gifts Sanaa received. Sanaa held a few bouquets in her hand as well.

"Well look at that," Mr. Cleophus smiled. "Let me help you ladies out."

Sanaa's favorite security guard was quick to come to Ms. Chase's aid. He relieved Ms. Chase first and then took some items from Chauncey. Sanaa held on to one bouquet; the two-dozen pink roses Kingston sent. Mr. Cleophus fell in line in front of the ladies and still managed to open and hold the door for them as they entered the garage.

"I saw you on the television, Ms. Chase, getting that award," Mr. Stanford sang. "I was so proud of you like you were my own daughter," Cleophus beamed. "I know that sounds silly," he smiled.

"No, Mr. Cleophus," Sanaa replied, pausing and turning to face him. "That's the sweetest thing anyone has ever said to me," Sanaa sighed, feeling a bit choked up by his sentiments. She leaned in and kissed Mr. Cleophus lightly on the cheek. "Thank you."

Now, it was Mr. Stanford who blushed.

"Let me help you get your stuff in the car," Cleophus smiled. He did just that, helped Sanaa get her belongings into the car. when he was done, Mr. Stanford tipped his hat and made his way back towards the entrance.

"We have a lot to do in the morning," Sanaa said. "Lots of new clients that we need to vet. So, go home, get some rest, and be ready to hit it hard in the morning."

"Yes ma'am," Chauncey replied. "See you in the morning."

"Stop grinning at me," Sana playfully chastised as she climbed into her car.

Chauncey laughed. She didn't need to say anything more.

Turning on the ignition, Sanaa waited until Chauncey was back into the building before backing out. She caught her reflection in the mirror. Sanaa was smiling, still. She really couldn't help it. There was something about Kingston that made Sanaa smile. It was scary though, uttering those three little words. As Sanaa pulled out of the garage and into traffic, she relived the moment when she got close to saying it. Even thinking about it made Sanaa's heart flutter and her gut churn. Those three little words were frightening. I love you meant surrender, loss of control, submission, commitment, feelings, emotions; all the things Sanaa had sworn off. *I love you* meant that she willingly acquiesced her position of strength and protection; something Sanaa thought she would never do, ever. But, in walked Kingston Wells. He swaggered into her life, refusing to be rejected, refusing to be dissuaded by Sanaa's hard exterior. Kingston refused to walk away from her. He persisted, he made it his business to be there, to be present and to make Sanaa understand that he had no intentions of going away, no matter how hard she pushed. And then, Kingston said those three little, magical, powerful, soul-snatching words... I love you.

Even reflecting on it, Sanaa felt verklempt, feeling the need to fan herself in the car although it wasn't hot in her car.

He loves me, Sanaa thought as she moved her car onto the interstate.

"He loves me," Sanaa whispered and then heard herself say it. Kingston Wells loved her.

The churning continued, and Sanaa felt a giddiness she'd never felt before; an overwhelming feeling she could hardly describe.

Sanaa spoke to her car, giving it an instruction.

"Call Kingston Wells."

"Calling Mr. Wells," the vehicle replied.

I can't believe I'm doing this, Sanaa thought. She felt her palms becoming clammy, and the beat of her heart begin to accelerate. Sanaa clutched the steering wheel harder as she heard Kingston's smooth voice come through her car's speakers.

"Hey there, beautiful," Kingston crooned.

Just hearing his voice gave Sanaa goosebumps and all the feels. Still, she felt choked up like the beat of her heart was too much and she couldn't fill her lungs with the air necessary to speak. But she did, and what Sanaa said next, changed the trajectory of her life.

"I love you, too."

The End

Thank you so much for reading Sanaa and Kingston's story. I would really appreciate it, especially if you enjoyed the story if you would leave a review on Amazon and Goodreads. For Indie authors, reviews are the lifeblood of our work. They give other readers insight into the story and greater visibility for the authors. Thanks in advance and I hope you will continue reading the Moore Friends Series with me!

If you haven't already, please check out,
Other Books Written by Celeste:

All That & Moore Series:
Hidden Missing Moore
I Am Moore
Teach Me Moore
Expect Moore
So Much Moore
Never Moore
I Found Moore

. . .

MOORE TO LOVE SERIES:
Stipulations
Gabriel's Melody
Temptations

MOORE FRIENDS SERIES:
Something New
A Love So New
Before I Fall
Lady Guardians Series:
Onyx Rides
Cruisin'

Coming Soon!

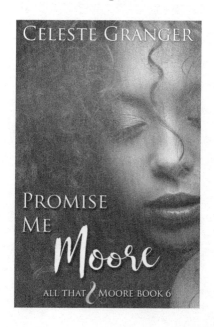

Want to be in the know? Subscribe to my newsletter to be a part of Celeste Granger's Tangled Romance!

HTTPS://LANDING.MAILERLITE.COM/WEBFORMS/LANDING/K2E1J4

Join my Reading Group! https://www.facebook.com/groups/1943300475969127/

Follow me on Facebook @ https://www.facebook.com/TheCelesteGranger/

Made in the USA
Middletown, DE
22 April 2025

74623837R00096